"HUMAN CHILD"

Come away, O human child! To the waters and the wild, With a faery hand in hand, For the world's more full of weeping than you can understand. Yeats.

Water

After her water broke they walked down to the stream, the dogs coming up to romp and frisk around them in excited anticipation.

The day was clear and bright after the passing of a short shower and in the sheer light and washed air all was lush and fresh, glinting and shining.

She carefully laid her clothes on the grassy bank and slipped naked into the clear pool, the coolness of the water causing her to take a sharp breath as her shoulders and breasts submerged.

Resting her back on the sandy bed in the shallows she hugged a boulder with each arm and stretched out, letting her legs and body float and sway in the thick glassy swirls of the flow, her breasts full and heavy glistening wetly as they rocked above the water, the brown nipples stretched by the press of milk and hard from the chill, the summit of her swollen belly appearing from time to time to show the distended navel and the ridge of downy black hair running down from it to become broken and woven by the ripples as it led to the darker shadow undulating deeper.

She relaxed and let the contractions come and go as they would, calmly accepting the stab of them, staying in the undercurrent of elation that each wave of pain twisted excruciatingly tighter.

He looked around, unconsciously registering the time and place; the sun high and dazzling in the vivid, dark blue of the almost

1

indigo sky, rarefied by the contrast of one stark white cloud rising from the top of the steep, solitary glen.

Spilling from the cloud a thin sparkling waterfall splashed down the rocks where the steep black crags that walled in the upper glen joined, and came away as the stream, flashing as it twisted its way down.

Bright thick purple heather and gleaming coarse yellow broom swayed in clumps and tufts at the foot of the black crags, then gave way to rough, dark green pastures that spread down, dappled with white patches that blinked here and there as the black faced sheep lifted and dipped their heads in their grazing huddles, the green expanse divided raggedly in two by the stream and carved up randomly like a simple jigsaw puzzle by the winding black stone walls.

Up the grassy slope from where he stood by the stream, meandering now for a while on flatter land, was the solid stone and slate roofed house, seemingly hewn from a single black rock, its small upper windows glinting and the slate of its roof shining; and by it, on the same level, a high leaning barn and a group of irregularly shaped farm buildings, also of stone and slate, formed around a stone paved courtyard, the whole huddle resting comfortably as it had come to settle of old.

Then, looking along the track that accompanied the stream into the haze far down the long, wild valley that eventually merged into the surrounding highlands, no sign of other humanity anywhere, he whispered to himself 'Beautiful' and turned and waded, dressed only in pants with belt and sheathed knife on, into the pool to stand between her calves.

He smiled gently down at her, and then going suddenly into himself, he became lost to all else, intently absorbing over and over the sight of her body, his awareness of her fertility so intensified by the ripeness of her swelling pregnancy that he could have rubbed her into his face like dark, moist topsoil.

Then, in awe of the weight of her flesh pressing against the rich lustre of the golden brown skin, with the melting dark patch between her legs clawing at his bowels, and transfixed by that face of faces that shone thrills into his being, the black hair undulated around it in the water, he knew more painfully than ever the unbearable longing that would only be satiated if he could somehow swallow her whole inside himself, that most intense desire of male human existence, insatiable in this life.

Watching his trance like engrossment, her gentle eyes softened by this outpouring of supra-human, transcendental passion, happily knowing that it was sparked and stoked by the quintessence of her femininity, she glowed in the aura of this thinly muscled man of hers with his shoulder length fair hair and finely featured face, only a few inches taller than herself, so intense and vibrant, kind and gentle also, and steeped in the wisdom acquirable only from nature - her peace, the seed of her fruit, her fulfilment.

His eyes came slowly back into focus, and smiling down at her again, he asked, 'How are you getting on, lass?'

She replied with a smile of her own, her lips so full and soft, the even strong teeth so white and clean, the pink gums so healthy that he had to join with her, and bent down to softly kiss her mouth.

Slowly they separated, the surge of the kiss strong in their breasts, and after gazing into the luminous, swirling pools of each other's eyes for all time, his seeing mellow brown, hers seeing pristine azure, he said softly and reluctantly, 'We'd better get on with it, lass.'

As if coming out of a dream she replied, 'Yes, it is coming now soon.'

'Cold?' he asked.

'No, it is good. It makes me feel alive. I am full of life.'

'That you are, lass,' he said. 'Right, let's try this. Place your feet on my ankles so you can push against my legs. That's it. Now I'll crouch down and grasp you round the neck. No, that's too far. We'll clasp each other's arms instead. Right, that's good. Perhaps your legs need to be higher up. You could hook them over my thighs. Yes, that's good. How is it for you? Can you brace yourself well?'

'Yes, it is good. I will have to move a lot,' she said, 'but, you know, in Spanish they say that the loads fit into their places on the way. It will be all right. Now, hold tight. Let me try pushing hard. Yes, that is good.'

'We'll battle this out together, lass,' he said. 'You'll have my all my strength to count on.'

'And you are so strong and so handsome, no?'

'All I am is yours, lass,' he replied with a soft smile.

At that moment she grimaced at a stab of pain, but without fuss. After the contraction passed she said, 'They are getting closer.'

'Right, hang in there, lass. I'm going up to the house for towels. I won't be long, so don't worry.'

'Yes, go. I will be all right.'

When he came back with a big pile of towels in his arms, she said, 'It is time.'

He got into the water, and moving between her legs, crouched down. She hooked her legs over his thighs and they clasped arms.

'When I must push,' she said, 'I will say "pull". Then you hold me.'

Nodding, he watched her expectantly, his body taut.

'Ready?' he asked.

'I am resting now,' she said.

Then after a few seconds she said, 'Now it begins. I will scream but it is nothing. Only to throw out the pain.'

Then he felt her begin to pull on his arms, and her weight press down on his thighs, and he tensed his muscles.

The pressure built up relentlessly until he had the full weight of her body hanging from his arms and thrusting down on his legs. He was surprised by her strength, so increased for this fulminating act of nature, and wondered how long he could hold out.

Then, her body completely strained, she yelled 'Pull!' the shout travelling up the glen like a shock wave.

The pressure rose to such a degree that he thought he might fall, but then adrenaline rushed to his head, and with more strength than he thought himself capable of he pulled until her whole body was hanging away from him, the two of them forming a taut hanging bow which dipped into the water.

Slowly the tension subsided and she rested on the bed of the stream, panting, her face trickling sweat.

'It was a good one,' she said.

'That it was, lass.'

'Now! Again!' she barked out hoarsely, and this time she jack-knifed into the hanging bow position with such speed that he rocked from the suddenness of her reaction.

'Aayayaay!' The scream blasted out so loudly from her that he could feel its vibrations on the skin of his face before it echoed up and out of the glen.

She sagged for an instant but snapped right back up again, almost bringing him down again on top of her, screeching 'Eeyaaaaa!'

Then a jerk, down and up, screaming again 'Eeyaaaaa!' more piercing and strained than before, eerily ringing in his ears, filling him with fear.

And, gasping, she yelled, 'It will come out now!', and jack-knifed again.

This time he hardly noticed the scream, so intent was he on holding her.

He could see that her hands and arms above where he was clasping them were becoming blue from lack of blood, and felt his feet slowly sinking into the sandy bed of the stream.

He looked down to see if they would hold, and instead saw something he didn't understand... a little black semicircle protruding from her crotch.

But then he saw that the water was washing itself away laced with threads of red, and an amazed elation came over him, forcing more strength into his stretched muscles, and with the words whistling out of his mouth, he yelled: 'The head is coming out.'

Sweat was trickling into his eyes and he had no way of wiping it off, so he blinked rapidly against the sting and shook his head sharply, his hair billowing out around his head spraying drops.

Then, with a colossal surge, she arched fully out of the water, her streaming body straining and trembling, the arc of her back with the round belly above forming a hump between his thighs and the taut cable of their linked arms, and with her face red and bulging, she held the position, pushing and pushing and pushing.

He looked quickly back down, and in that instant a little waxed and blood streaked body slipped out of her, trailing a fleshy rope behind, splashed into the water and sank onto the bed of the stream.

She sagged now, completely exhausted, and he gently let her slip back into the water then hurriedly groped for the little body.

Finding first the umbilical cord, he pulled it in until he could see little arms and legs waving about in the bloody water, which quickly swept clear to let him see that the baby was quite calm, and seemed only to be trying to swim, so, reaching under the surface, he wiped off the remaining strands of blood and mucus sticking to the little body, and taking it under its arms, lifted it out of the water and held it up to her, streaming, the umbilical cord swinging between them.

'It is a boy,' she said. 'How beautiful he is.'

'It's a boy?' he asked uncomprehendingly, for the first time truly realising what he had in his hands, and turned the baby to face him.

Staring in wonder, he focused automatically on the seemingly disproportionately long hose like penis sticking almost straight out of the compact little body.

'Well, he seems well equipped in that area anyway,' he said.

She smiled and said, 'They all do when they are babies.'

'Do they, though? I don't suppose we Scots have much to boast about as far as that's concerned, but maybe your Gitano blood has more to offer.'

'So the Gitano men like to believe, but who knows.'

But he was lost again in the sight of the baby, the skin so white and translucent against the contrasting crest of jet black hair running along the ridge of the head.

Huge milky blue eyes below thick dark eyebrows and shadowed by long ashen eyelashes were wide open and staring here and there with intense interest.

'You'd think he can see everything,' he said. 'Well, why shouldn't he be interested in the blurry blobs he's seeing for the first time? God, he's so beautiful.'

Then, squinting amusingly at the baby, he said playfully to it, 'You're not very big though, are you?'

She had been watching his entranced gazing with gentle pride.

'Don't worry, he is big enough. You can weigh him after, but now you must make him breathe.'

'What? O, yes! Of course, I won't spank him, though,' he said, and after a moment's thought, he covered the baby's mouth with his own, and sealing it well with his lips, he blew softly.

Pulling his head back he looked at the baby with concern, but nothing happened, so he covered the baby's mouth with his own again and blew several times very gently.

Just when he was about to give up, the baby gasped and spluttered, let out one thin wail, then went on staring.

'That's him on his way, then,' he said, and went on hurriedly to cover his relief, 'Hell of a thing for a baby to be born. All they must want to do is to get right back into the warm, quiet womb. Well, he'll both hate and love what's ahead, but that's life, and who would miss it?'

'You did well,' she said in admiration for his sure instincts. 'Now you must cut the cord.'

'Right,' he said, taking his knife out of its sheath on his belt.

'I'd better sterilise this first,' he went on, and looked around in doubt.

'Come here. Give him to me,' she said. 'I have been wanting him so badly. See how I give him his first treat.'

She confidently took the little wet body, and cradling it in her right arm, guided the head to the nipple of her left breast, which the baby took eagerly and sucked at strongly.

'Aah, how good,' she murmured.

Unable to tear himself away he remained fast in the water gazing in baffled wonder at the beauty of this mother with suckling child - the mother, his woman; the child, his first son.

From a tight knot in the centre of his chest he felt a wave of compressed hot love ribbon out, spreading as it went to envelop them both, and he thought, 'I can feel this passion so intensely, but there is no way I could ever express it. I have no way to let them know the strength of it. Oh how I wish I could, but it is beyond human ability. It is spirit soaring beyond flesh.'

His eyes watered and he turned brusquely away.

He went up to a lean-to against the house, open to the stream below, where there was a whetting wheel, and sitting on the stool in front of it, pedalled and pressed the blade of his knife to the turning stone wheel, making sparks fly like galaxies; then he lit the oil lamp standing on the rough wooden table beside him and drew the blade backward and forward in the hottest part of the flame for a few seconds.

Looking up, he noticed that her belly was still round and hard, and frowning uncertainly he called to her, 'Don't you become flat again after the baby is born?'

She was absorbed in the sight of the baby suckling at her breast and started slightly.

'There is another one,' she said.

'What?' he gasped, incredulously, and then, in awe, whispered, 'I can't believe I'm so lucky! How God blesses me.'

'He is good to me too, you know?' She said gently, seeing how exalted he was. 'He gave me you.'

'Yes, yes,' he hurriedly said, 'but your nature, your spirit is heavenly. You are far nearer to God than anyone I've ever known.'

'It is just that I am woman and can make life which makes you feel that way.'

'You see, you know you're special,' he said, calming down and going back into the stream.

'Anyway, you're certainly special to me, lass. Right, I'm going to cut this little fellow's cord. I've sharpened and disinfected the knife.'

Bending over her, he weighed the cord in his left hand a few times, then pulled it tight, and placing the cutting edge of the knife against it a little way from the baby's belly, with one fast slice he cut it.

'Not much blood,' he said. 'Now hold him up a bit and I'll tie the knot,' which he did neatly so that it was tight against the little belly.

'How's that?' he asked.

'Very good,' she said.

'Yes, it looks good. What now?'

'We wait. See, it starts again,' she said, as a spasm made her shudder.

'Here, let me take the baby.'

She disengaged the baby from her nipple and handed him up. He took the baby and rocked him proudly in his arms for a while, and the baby stared up at him wide eyed.

Then he waded to the bank, spread out a towel and laid the baby safely on it.

The dogs, who had watched everything sitting and lolling on the bank of the stream, now cautiously approached the baby, and after a few sniffs, set to licking him vigorously.

'That's my girls. Good girls, good girls,' he said in the usual authoritative but kind voice he used to talk to them.

'You girls warm the little fellow up.' And turning to her, he said, 'The best thing for a new born baby is a good massage, and none better than from the strong, rough tongues of the dogs.'

She was already in pain and breathing in rapid gusts, through which she managed to say haltingly, 'Yes, that is very good. Now come, I need you.'

'Right,' he said, and waded over to her, and they locked together as before.

'I hope this time it will be more easy. Take me!' she exclaimed. He quickly grabbed her up, and right away she doubled over, swinging at both their arms' length, water running off the dusky skin of her half submerged bare body, and her dark, long hair spreading downstream around her curved, soft flanks.

Exhaling a long drawn out groan, she sagged for a few seconds then arched away again, groaning.

Then, 'Gasp, gasp, gasp, gasp, gasp. Aaaaay, *Madre Bendita*... Aaaaay, *Madre*... Aaaaay, *Madre*!'

And sagging, pant, pant, pant, gasping out, 'Is it coming?'

He was so intent on her throes that he didn't understand at first, but quickly looked down and saw that the water was murky with slimy, clotted blood, and he thought, 'Oh no, don't let it go wrong now, please, please. Don't let anything happen to her, please.' He looked up quickly to see if she was all right.

She sagged again.

'It's very bloody,' he said as calmly as he could.

'It, gasp, is the first, gasp, afterbirth.'

'Oh!' he exhaled with relief. 'Thank God!'

Automatically, he looked down and up, then quickly down again.

'Here comes something!' he shouted. But she couldn't answer because she had thrust up and was using all her strength to push.

Straining against her pull, he continued looking down, and, o, wonder, the little round ball of a head emerged, this time covered in blond fuzz.

'Looks like a tennis ball this time,' he said, but she had gone limp, and said, with agony in her voice, 'I cannot do it.'

'Right, keep calm, lass,' he said. 'There, there, lass. Easy, easy, my love.'

'I cannot do it,' she said again.

'OK, lass. Listen! The babe will choke if we don't get it out now.'

'I cannot do it,' she said, and tears welled up in her eyes and spilled down her cheeks. 'I cannot do it,' she sobbed.

In her weakness he became strong; and filled with the power that comes only to succour one more important to one than oneself, he said calmly and with absolute confidence, 'Lass, I'll let you down. Now hug those two boulders again. That's it. Now, I'm going to get down so that I can help by pulling the baby.' And he lay face down on the surface of the water, his head up between her thighs, holding onto the stream bed with his hands, his legs drifting down stream for a moment, then his feet digging in.

'Right, I'm set, lass,' he said, lifting his face out of the water. 'Now, hook your legs over my shoulders. That's it. Come on now, lass. We're nearly there. Start pushing.'

His decisiveness calmed her, and tightening her grip on the boulders, she gave a tentative push.

'Harder, lass,' he exhorted her, and she tried again, her stomach muscles screaming from being so overworked.

When he saw new determination on her face he let go of the stream bed with his hands, and holding against the current with his feet, took a deep breath and ducked his face into the water.

Not being able to see much, he felt until his hands cupped the little head, and with his fingertips he felt her brim straining hard around it.

Just then the brim relaxed and the head shot out of his hands as it was pulled back inside her.

Raising his head above the water, he saw her take a deep breath and her face turn purple as she started pushing again.

Down went his face, and up between her legs, feeling her brim with his fingertips, he cupped the little head when it re-emerged.

The head started to press into his hands, and very slowly and carefully he pulled it. He could feel that she had relaxed but he didn't ease up his pull on the little head, and then he felt a new pressure and knew she was pushing again.

Gently he pulled a little harder.

Suddenly the baby slid out so fast and unexpectedly that it slithered out of his hands and was lost to him in the murky red water.

Straining to hold his breath for a second longer he thrashed around, desperately groping for the baby, lightheaded now from lack of oxygen, when, suddenly, feeling the umbilical cord, he grasped it and pulling it to him, let all his air out, shot his head out of the water, and sucked in an enormous breath.

She lay in the water panting, her face covered in sweat, her body gone completely limp.

'Do you have it?' she rasped fearfully.

'It's coming now,' he said as he lifted the umbilical cord out of the water and the little body bobbed onto the surface.

He took it under its arms, lifted it out, and gave it a searching look.

'What is it?' she asked.

'What is it? Oh, of course. It's another boy. Look.'

And he bent down to show her.

'He also is beautiful,' she said with a beatific smile.

'This one is a lot bigger,' he said, as he took in the light golden tan of the skin, set off strikingly by the yellow fuzz on the round scalp, and the furry, sandy eyebrows and wispy golden eyelashes.

The face was wrinkled like an old man's and the baby was sound asleep.

Feeling he would cry from the let down and relief, choking, he said,

'Slept through the whole thing, this little fellow did,' and, lifting the baby's face to his, he put his lips over the baby's mouth and blew.

The baby's eyes flew wide open, the milky black pupils gazing at the middle distance, still asleep.

Sucking in a sharp breath, the baby began breathing regularly and the eyes closed again.

'Right, here goes the umbilical cord,' he said. He edged away from her with his left arm around the baby till the cord tightened, he took hold of it with his left hand, withdrew the knife from its sheath on his belt with his right hand, sliced and quickly tied the knot with hands encircling the little body.

'Another good job,' he said.

Then he started to laugh. 'You little beauty, you,' he said, laughing again; and holding the baby out at arm's length he started to dance a jig, splashing water all over her and the dogs and the first baby.

'You little darlings,' he said. He leaned down for the baby on the bank, and with one in the crook of each arm he danced out of the stream and whirled and spun on the grassy verge shouting, 'Hey, hey, hey! Hey, hey, hey!'

She looked at him with mock ferocity as he wheeled away up the slope kicking his feet out and pirouetting past the house, singing out 'hey, hey, hey' as he went, his pants clinging to his body and shining wetly.

Then, straight back down the slope, circling round and round, letting his elbows and the babies in them be pulled up and away, and swept finally onto his knees on the bank above her, where he remained panting with bowed head.

She held her scolding frown for a second then laughed warmly and said, 'I wish I could dance with you.'

'Lass, you'll dance your feet off in good time. Right now, you rest,' he said looking down at the babies' faces. The first one was staring around gurgling happily. The second one was sound asleep.

'This little golden one must be washed,' he said, and placing the first baby back on its towel, he dipped the second baby in the water, holding him with one hand and rubbing him with the other.

'Don't you want to come out?' he asked her.

'I'm waiting to empty out all the afterbirth. I want to come out all clean.'

He dried off the second baby and laying him beside his brother on the towel in the warm sun, called over the dogs. They came smiling, with glistening eyes and tails wagging so hard that their whole hindquarters swayed. After sniffing the new arrival they set to licking him so hard that he rocked from side to side, but he didn't wake.

Going over to her he sat in the shallow water by her head, and bending over to kiss her long and softly on the mouth.

'You did so well,' he said as he drew back. 'I'm so proud of you. I love you more than you can know.'

She smiled happily. 'Life is so good. This world is so beautiful and you are so good for me. You make my spirit fly. Look at my spirit flying!' she cried, pointing to a white osprey soaring high up the glen.

'You'll fly, all right, but out of this water and into the sun,' he said.

'Let me finish. Go and look after the babies.'

'I can see they're fine. But I'll tell you what I am going to do. If you are all going to sunbathe naked, then so am I.' He stepped out of the water, stripped off his pants and shorts and threw them in a pile on the grass.

Completely naked he got down, and butting the dogs with his head, crawled through them and lay between the two babies, the dogs continuing to lick the second baby.

Lifting himself on one elbow he looked down at the second baby; then, reaching back with his other arm, he brought the first baby over, and laying him beside his younger brother, he examined them both.

'The little brother is the older brother and the big brother is the younger brother,' he said, looking over to her between the dog's legs. Then went on, 'Oh! they're so beautiful; each one's colouring is so distinctive. One black and white, the other tan and blond, one wide awake and one sound asleep.' Leaning over them, he hugged one into each shoulder.

Wanting his attention for themselves, the dogs nuzzled in, so that after a bit he said, 'Back, girls. Back. Back now. Sit. Lie.' They spread out around him, sitting and lying, each in its own way, and he looked over at her again.

'I am clean now,' she said.

'Good. Come on out,' he said, laying the babies back on the towel and getting up.

She rose out of the water stiffly, her glistening body streaming water, and stood in the shallows swaying unsteadily. He jumped over to her and caught her by an arm. She leaned against him.

'I am so weak,' she said, and he put his arm around her and drew her tightly into himself.

'Come, I'll lift you,' he said. Leaning over, he swept her legs out from under her and carried her onto the grassy verge.

'Try to stand here,' he said, and put her feet on the ground.

'I am fine,' she said. 'It was only when I stood up.'

He held her with one hand and reached down with the other to pick up a large towel.

'Hold on to me,' he said. 'I'm going to rub you down.' And wrapping her in the rough towel, he rubbed her briskly all over from shoulders to feet.

When he took the towel away her body was rosy and glowing.

'Now,' he said, 'sit here beside the babies in the sun.' He eased her down so she folded cross-legged onto the ground with her body bowing over her jutting knees and her head hanging above her ankles, her hands overlapped on her crotch, her hair curtaining loosely around.

After a few seconds she took a fresh towel to dry her hair, first rubbing backwards and forwards above and behind her head, her breasts bouncing and swaying, the dark patches under her arms blinking. Then with a sweeping motion she brought her hair down over her body so that it trailed on the ground beyond her feet. Leaving her head hanging forward, she rubbed the hair between the towel fabric with the palms of her hands. Finally, she threw her head back, the long black hair arcing up from her legs high over in the air to fall on her back, then wrapped it in the towel, making a neat turban that sat firmly on her head.

She sat saying nothing, looking straight ahead without focusing, concentrating on the warmth of the sun seeping into her body.

He put his arms round her, trying to warm her with his body.

'Feeling better?' he asked.

'Yes,' she said unblinkingly. 'I am suddenly sad, and because I am tired the sadness is stronger than I am.'

'It's the aftermath, lass,' he said.

'I will lie down,' she said, and lay on the grass, the towel pillowing her head, and closing her eyes she offered her face and body to the sun.

'The sun will heal you, lass. Let it warm your soul.'

He walked up to and into the house, almost dragging his legs from the sagging relief his whole body felt, and reappeared with two silk scarves, one blue and one yellow. Arriving back at the still, lying group, he covered the first born baby with the blue scarf and the second born one with the yellow scarf.

Then he lay still beside her and held her hand.

After a few minutes he felt her breathing become regular, and looking at her face he saw that she was asleep; so, after checking the babies on her other side and seeing that they were both asleep, he closed his eyes also.

Watching the orange-red honeycomb pattern that the sunlight made as it shone through his eyelids until it faded, he drifted into that hypnotic pre-sleep state when thought thinks for itself, and found himself looking down on the four of them lying immobile on the ground with the dogs sprawling about them, hearing his mind's voice saying... 'A male and a female human, Mature in flesh, In lusty health and prime physique, Different races, Two faces of the beauty of Man, Tones and hues of colour mingling, And between them the palette blending newly, In the babies of their bodies...'

Trailing off, he dozed without completely losing awareness.

Thus they lay in the still warm peace of the golden afternoon while all nature dozed and the sun wheeled above the isolated glen...

Stretching, one of the dogs raised itself onto its haunches, lifted one leg and scratched its ribs. Then it yawned and groaned.

Another one opened its eyes and looked around without moving its head, which lay sideways on the ground.

Birds began to chirp again and a slight breeze gently waved the stalks of the scattered yellow dandelions.

He sat up and gazed straight ahead sleepily, looked down at the three sleeping bodies beside him, the babes hidden beneath their bright scarves, then looked all around.

Yes, it was real. Really, unreally, real.

The earth was a warm bowl in the centre of which he sat. The sky was around and above and below, the vast reaches of space beyond turning violet. And it had happened. They were born. They had materialised out of the light loving waters into the breathing breeze of the air.

Everything was buoyed on sparkling light, and he was inside himself, and everything was inside him inside everything else. The earth was inside him, the sky was inside the earth, space was a small crystal ball inside the sky, and their four bodies were one inside the crystal ball.

He smiled, feeling he would levitate, rose onto his feet and floated over to the stream. Bending over a pool his shimmering face looked back at him. He smiled again, lovingly, for in himself he saw all of creation. Then lowered his lips to the water, sucked it up and drank.

Getting up he moved softly over to the pile of towels. Taking up a towel he carried it over to the three sleeping beings and lovingly spread it over her sleep softened and soothed body, and sat down.

She rolled away from him onto her side, taking the towel with her in her arms and curling up her legs.

Fulfilled, he looked at her curving back and round, swelling buttocks, with that dark triangular patch disappearing between the behind tops of her thighs.

Rolling again onto her back, leaving the towel behind, she looked up into his eyes and they smiled warmly and lazily at each other.

Lifting her arms up, she rolled the back of her head against the grass, arched her neck up, and stretched her whole body.

'I am like new after that siesta,' she said, relaxing her body again. 'Now, let me see my babies.' And on hands and knees she crawled over and on top of them.

'Look, you have covered them so beautifully with my scarves. Very good.'

'Yes,' he said back. 'I didn't want them to get sunburned. Your brown skin can take it, but theirs is too new.'

'I will make shade for them with my body. Now, let me peek at them,' she said as she pulled back the blue scarf covering one of the little bulks.

'*Ay, que lindo!*' Yes, it is the little, dark one. See how he looks at me with those enormous eyes. And the skin so white, and that hair so black standing up on his head. He is so pure.'

She bent and rubbed her nose against his. 'My love, my love,' she crooned.

'I think he will have blue eyes like yours. Now, let me see my other love,' she said, and slowly peeled back the yellow scarf covering the other little bulk.

'No! no! no!' she said. 'How precious he is. Look, he sleeps. Like a little hero. So strong. So colourful. Copper skin and gold hair. I will stroke his fuzzy head.' And placing an elbow on the ground at either side of his face, she rubbed his head with both hands.

Standing up she tied a scarf round the top of each of her knees so that they trailed down the outside of her calves, brightening her presence and making her every move like little lightning flashes.

'Now I will feed them,' she said, getting down over the babies, one hand supporting her from the outside side of each of their heads, moving her swinging breasts forward over their faces.

Holding her body up on her right arm, she used her left hand to guide the nipple of her right breast into the dark baby's mouth, who took it gingerly and began slowly sucking, at last shutting his eyes.

Next she balanced on her left arm and with her right hand moved the nipple of her left breast towards the light baby's mouth. He continued sleeping, so she poked his lips with the nipple, then, tickled his mouth with it. But still he did not wake, so she grasped her breast and squeezed it, forcing a jet of warm milk to spray down on his face. At this his eyes shot open and she was able to see them for the first time.

'I think this one will have black eyes,' she said, holding the nipple off for a moment, then letting it be sucked into the baby's mouth, as he closed his eyes again.

Holding herself up on one hand she took the towel off her head, tossed it aside, let her head hang down to rest her neck, and her hair fell like a curtain over the babies.

Through the hair he watched the two babies suckling from the hanging breasts of their mother on all fours above them and thought: 'Romulus and Remus.'

As though having read his mind, she asked from inside her hair, 'How are we going to call them?'

'Lass, you read my mind, didn't you?'

'I think so.'

'But you didn't read the words.'

'No.'

'Well, lass, I had thought we should wait to get to know them a bit before deciding, like I do with my dogs. But seeing you feeding them like that, the names Romulus and Remus came straight into my mind, and when something like that happens, so freely, it should be considered. What do you think?'

'*Romulo y Remo*,' she said softly in Spanish, savouring the sounds. 'Romulus and Remus of Rome, who were suckled by a she-wolf. Romulo y Remo. I like them much. Remember, we the Gitanos are the people of Romany. It is like a sign from this marvellous day.'

'Well, we don't have much else to do with Rome... but then what do Scottish-Spanish, Highland-Gitano have to do with each other anyway? That's settled, then,' he said, laughingly. 'Romy and Remy!'

She raised her head and looked round at him, her hair falling apart to reveal her nose and eyes, and asked him, 'Will anything ever be so perfect again?'

'No,' he said. 'It never will. But there will be other moments which will be heartfelt in their way.'

'It frightens me,' she said. 'Can it be we will have to pay for being so happy today?'

'I know how you feel,' he said. 'All we can do is revel in the now. Leave it all in heaven's hands, lass, and be happy.'

'Amen,' she said. Then gaily again: 'Papi,' she said. 'You are now a Papi.'

'And you are Mother.'

'Mami. I am Mami. We are a Papi and a Mami. That is how I called my father and mother when I was a little girl,' she said, and after a pause... 'And I still do.'

'My father used to call my mother "Mother", he said. 'But my mother always called him by his first name. Pity they can't be here. I think I will go over and pay my respects,' and he got up.

'Wait. We are all going to go so that your parents can see their grandchildren.'

She gently released her nipples from the baby's mouths and sat beside them.

'I will take one,' he said.

'No. You will take both of them, so you can present them in an appropriate manner, and with pride.'

He held out his arms and she placed the dark baby in his right arm. 'This one is Romulus, Romy,' she said, 'because he came first.'

Then she placed the light baby in his left arm and said, 'And this is Remus, Remy.'

Leaning back slightly, he hugged the babies into his chest with their heads on his shoulders in his hands. And, when he turned, their faces looked back at her - dark, slight Romulus staring all around, and light, large Remus sound asleep.

'They look so divine,' she murmured.

'Right, let's go to our own little graveyard,' he said. And they wandered, alive and free in their nakedness along the grassy verge of the stream, the scarves around her knees blinking brightly, the dogs, looking dressed by comparison, trailing lazily along behind...

(What I wouldn't give to be capable of filming what you have just seen! ... B)

Babies and Boys

Thus, then, were born Romy and Remy.

The night of their birth, in their shared crib, in the dark, John and Emilia find Romy and Remy glowing, an effervescent green semicircle covering them both, but closer, from their faces, a blue like the deep sky from Romy, and a yellow like the fiery sun from Remy, and the effect of ecstatic delight caused by the lights on John and Emilia makes silent tears of bliss spill out of their eyes and run down their cheeks.

They grow up with each other in the beautiful isolation of the glen and surrounding highlands: Romy, dark of hair, dark blue of eyes and white of skin, slight and slim, sensitive and spiritual; Remy, fair of hair, black of eyes and burnished of body, burly and physical, aware and protective. They speak Spanish and English equally as easily.

For their christening Emilia's Gitano family clan come from Central Europe in horse and ox-drawn vehicles, with much flurry and excitement at their arrival several weeks after.

All kinds of events and festivities take place, both Gitano and Scottish: Flamenco dancing on tapping shoes and Highland flings on toe tips, bagpipes and swirling kilts, guitars and clapping and swirling dresses, horses prancing, border collies herding sheep, bonfires and fireworks, wrestling and caber tossing, put shots and javelins, flame throwers and jugglers, all ending in the great celebration of the christening itself , with full Gitano Catholic garb, in the stream at the place where Romy and Remy were born.

Romy shows early signs of being unusual. He is uncannily intelligent, comprehending and caring, with sage and hermit like ways. He won't eat meat and is overwhelmed by saddening things, which make him hysterical and pass out.

Remy is Romy's protector and takes into himself the pains Romy can't bear, often bringing Romy back from unconsciousness, holding him in his arms on the floor until both boys are in a trance like state of total concentration, absolutely isolated from their surroundings. Frozen in each other's clutch, their concentration becomes so fierce that John and Emilia know they are no longer with them. They have gone into their own world far away, an invisible shield enveloping them.

...

So they lie there, stiff in each other's embrace, eyes closed.

John looks over at Emilia.

'We must wait,' she says tensely.

'How long?' John asks.

'I don't know. For a few minutes,' she whispers.

As they watch on in the loud silence, they start to feel their tension ease. Their muscles begin to relax and sleepiness overcomes them. With drooping eyelids they stare straight ahead. Their heads begin to nod and their eyes close.

John struggles against the force that has been draining his consciousness from him. He tries with all the power of his will to open his eyes but cannot.

Then, as though a light has been turned on, he is suddenly fully awake. The room has come back to life. Emilia is looking around and Romy and Remy are now lying side by side.

Romy looks at them with large shimmering eyes. *'Hola, Papi,'* he says. *'Hola, Mami.* Remy has taken it. It is all right now'

....

When they are ten years old Romy and Remy go to a small coeducational school within driving distance occupying a castle looking out over the dark, thrilling North Sea.

The school is an expensive one, tough and harsh for Romy, but with every facility for learning, as well as for sports and games - rugby, cricket, hockey, squash, fencing, boxing, swimming, and there is small boat sailing on the sea

...

Desperately and profoundly they want to disappear, to run away, to be anywhere but there, to do anything other than this. Never have they felt so strongly the desire for something as they do for this. It is the first time they truly want something, the agonising yearning for this cup to pass from them. But they know there is no choice. Like an execution it will proceed.

...

Here they meet the very self-willed, determined, temperamental, beautiful, sensitive, devoted Cherry, of their own age, who is the daughter of the headmaster and his wife.

...

There is a woman talking earnestly to a little girl who is standing on the arm of a large sofa.

'Now, Cherry,' the woman is saying. 'Stop all this fuss. You will go to school no matter what you say or do, so get down from there.'

The woman is Fiona, her mother and the headmaster's wife.

Cherry puts her hands on her hips and stamps her right foot on the arm of the sofa. 'I will not go. I will never go. I know more than any of the others. They are all ugly and stupid and I'm not going near them. Never!' And she looked down her nose at her mother defiantly.

'Cherry, you're driving me crazy. Get down from there. If you won't go by yourself I will carry you.'

Cherry stamps her foot on the sofa arm again, her face flushing, and says, 'How dare you humiliate me in any such way,' her small delicate nose scrunching up, her full lips pouting, her large green eyes flashing from within long light eyelashes, her dark red eyebrows furrowing and her glossy deep red hair tossing about as she throws her head around arrogantly.

Romy and Remy watch her in fascination. They have never thought to contradict adults and don't believe it can be done, yet here it is.

...

With Romy and Remy, Cherry becomes the third member of the sublime, spiritual 'Human Child' trinity

....

Kneeling and awkwardly clasping hands in front of them they glance shyly at each other a few times. Then their glances begin to hold, each time for longer, until they stare fixedly at one shining point above their bunched hands. Warmth radiates through their bodies and they feel light and free and happy. Entranced and enchanted they stare on and on, their life forces being gently drawn out of them and absorbed by the shining focal point. Suddenly the point blooms into a glowing ball and then collapses back onto itself, fusing to become a dense luminary of pure white light. A thrill runs through their beings and they know they have become one and that they are one with everything.

...

After this Romy performs his first healing. A senior boy with authority incessantly and cruelly abuses Romy until one time, when Romy has just passed out, Remy jumps on his back, gets him round the throat and chokes him unconscious onto the floor.

...

Remy lets go of Cameron and rolls onto the floor knocking into Romy's body. He lifts himself up onto his knees and seeing Romy's catatonic trance leaps up and begins circling the two bodies. He stands over Romy for a long time, and then lying down beside him rolls on top of Romy's stiff, staring body. He puts his arms around Romy, and, closing his eyes tightly, concentrates with all the power of his thought on finding a passage into Romy's brain.

All is still except for the slowly circling form of Cherry.

A sudden green flash lights up everything and Remy rolls off Romy and lies on his back, pale and panting, his strength depleted.

Romy sits up and looks around. 'Remy, I'm back,' he says.

Remy says, 'Let me rest for a while, Romy.'

'Yes, Remy, you rest,' Romy says, leaning down and kissing Remy's forehead. 'I'm going to wake Cameron up.'

Romy goes over to Cameron and kneels down in front of his face, which lies sideways on the floor. He looks pityingly at the lifeless face for a long time then rolls the limp body onto its back, and sitting down with legs crossed he takes Cameron's head into his lap so that he is looking down at Cameron's face from above and behind it. Placing his right palm over the back of his left hand so that his hands and fingers take the shape of wings, he places them on Cameron's head, and closing his eyes, he rocks slowly back and forward, gently humming a single, low, reverberating note.

Cameron's irises roll down from his forehead and he stares into the distance then looks into Romy's smiling eyes which glow with compassion. Cameron's gaze lingers for a long time on the glistening pools of Romy's eyes, slowly and inexorably being drawn into their peace.

At last Cameron croaks, 'Romy, I think I love you.'

...

Romy, Remy and Cherry become aware then that Romy is able to heal spiritually, and to cure psychological trauma.

The headmaster, who is also a Minister, is a brutal man and unwell mentally. Romy heals him immediately after healing Cameron.

...

'What on earth is going on here?' Allan's harsh voice suddenly startles them all and they turn to him in fright. He stands there fuming, his face swollen and bright red from pent up anger.

'Break ended half an hour ago!' he shouts. 'Didn't you hear the bell? Didn't you hear the bloody bell? Cameron, didn't you hear the bell, boy!?'

'No sir.'

Allen makes a lightning move and his arm blurs through the air and hits Cameron on the side of his head, knocking him over and causing blood to trickle from his ear.

'Perhaps that will help you to hear the bell from now on. And what's all this disgusting hugging and smiling about? Have you all gone mad?'

'But, Sir,' Cameron says, looking up from the ground, 'we've decided to make this the best school in the land. We're not going to be cruel to each other any more.'

'Really,' Allan says scathingly. 'And where did all this come from? You'll do that over my dead body. I'll nip this in the bud if it's the last thing I do. Come on, where did all this come from?'

'It's the right thing. It's a good thing,' Romy pipes up.

'Oh, so you're the troublemaker are you, Romy? You little bugger,' Allan hisses, and moves swiftly in Romy's direction with his hand raised. But Remy darts in front of him and knocks him to the ground.

Grovelling on the ground, his face crimson and bursting, he mumbles and spits out horribly: 'You little buggers. You little shits. By God, you'll pay for this!' But as he is getting to his knees, a frightened, shocked look comes over his face, and he says, 'Oh, I have a pain under both my arms. Oh, it's moving across my chest. Oh, oh God, I'm going to die.' He doubles over, hugging his chest. 'Oh,' he groans. 'Oh.' His face begins to turn purple and sweat pours down it and over his neck. 'I have to get my clothes off," he says in panic. And he tears at his clerical collar, pulls his jacket off, then rips at his shirt till it comes away in shreds and his heavy, kneeling body is bared to the waist.

'Look into my eyes!' Romy suddenly commands him. 'You will look into my eyes. You will look into my eyes.'

Allan looks desperately at Romy, his hopeless bloated face showing disbelief and exasperation at what Romy is doing.

'Look into my eyes!' Romy commands again in a still firmer tone. 'Look!' he orders and Allan's eyes meet his for a second, then shy away.

'Look!' Romy orders again. 'Look!' And Allan's eyes return to his and stay for a few seconds.

'Longer. Deep into my eyes,' Romy insists. 'Straight into my eyes.'

Allan in his agony is unable to fight it any longer and looks dumbly into Romy's eyes, at first seeing nothing, but then slowly becoming immersed in the blue pools of shimmering light which draw on his inner being, slowly withdrawing it and absorbing it.

Allan now gazes in fascination, seeing in the pools of blue light eddying currents and swirling clouds beyond which there is a darker blue glow which Allan knows he has to reach. He knows he has to get through the currents and clouds and into the blue velvety glow, and he wills himself on, wills himself forward, wills himself through the layers of mist that dim the blue glow; and Romy pulls him on with all his will, his awareness completely focussed on pulling Allan deeper into the blue glow. They are completely isolated from their surroundings, and their whole existence is in each other's eyes.

'Leave them,' Cherry says sharply under hear breath with so much authority that Fiona is checked.

'Cherry, what are you talking about? He'll die,' she too under her breath.

'Leave them,' Cherry says again. 'Romy is looking after him.'

'What can a little boy do? What can Romy know about heart attacks?'

'Instead of making such a fuss, Mum, why don't you just watch for a moment?'

A great peace comes over Allan's countenance and he stares on into Romy's eyes in rapture. The sweat drips less and less, and the heaving of the bare chest slows and relaxes, and slowly his whole figure settles down and is still and at rest.

His arms, bit by bit, sink down from his chest to hang at his sides and his face radiates in crystal clarity around the glowing ruddy cheeks; and he stares on and on into Romy's eyes.

'Rest now,' Romy whispers. 'Let go of your body. Release all your muscles and fill all your being with peace.' Romy places his hand on Allan's shoulder. 'Feel the peace going through my hand into your being. Take it all and know love. Fill your soul with this love and you will know peace and joy, and you will be fulfilled.'

Allan's whole body sags on his kneeling legs, his head sinks deeper onto his chest, his eyelids close over his tired eyes and tears trickle from their edges and run down his cheeks.

After taking and pressing Romy's hand firmly to his lips Allan raises his head, and holding out Romy's hand in front of his face to look devotedly at it, says in a faraway voice: 'Out of the mouths of babes and infants I have heard at last, and for the for the first time have ever heard. I, a Minister of God, who thought he knew God's will and commands. Who thought he was holier than others. I was blind and now can see, deaf and now can hear, senseless and now can feel.'

...

The school changes to a loving place, but Romy goes home.

...

So Romy stays at home, stays in the warm security of the house that is like a womb for him, and spends long hours walking with the dogs in the fields and among the sheep. Idles along the sparkling, gurgling stream and rises to the top of the glen to look at the infinite distance of evanescent sky above and beyond the layers of hills. Immerses himself in the woods and feels protected and safe in their embrace. Fascination accompanies his every moment and he continually ponders with awe the ways and beauties of nature. The world seems eternally far away and unreal and the stars and the seasons roll around and about him and he gains in knowledge far beyond his years.

As imperceptibly as Spring lingeringly lights up Winter until the day comes when incredulously we see that all is green and thickly leafed and all is blooming and all is blossoming and we realise that Summer is upon us and Summer is within us and if we do not respond and come fully alive it will be over before we realise it, so too, by and by, did Romy and Remy became fully adolescent - supple and lithe as sapling trees, radiating clean health and latent spiritual and physical power, knowing each other's thoughts.

...

Because he accidentally cuts Emilia, Romy stabs himself in the belly with the same knife and sinks down unconscious. Emilia swiftly moves in, and, seeing that the wound is in the muscle on the outside of the abdomen and does not affect any organs, she removes the blade and staunches the bleeding and disinfects the wound and places a pressure bandage on it. She then looks pleadingly at Remy, but Remy shakes his head. She gives him another look of agony. Then Remy slowly, tiredly takes hold of Romy, not to bring him back this time but for them both to leave this world together.

Cherry is rushed to their side from the school by John. She senses their leaving.

Cherry's song for Romy and Remy as they lie unconscious makes Remy turn from leaving life with Romy to fighting to bring them both back.

...

'In mother's spirit speak I, No love in all the universe alike to mine is nigh, No wish of mother for her child to fly, No love of sister for soul sister's yearning cry, Or love to love of one brother for the other so does sigh. Yea Remy, love thou Romy stronger than strong, But let thyself too be loved for long, For love us three requires, To light and burn as bright as pyres.'

...

The three beautiful now grown children, exhausted, are lain down side by side to sleep, Cherry between the two boys.

This experience, which causes Cherry to finally fall completely in love with Remy, awakes first, and sits up between him and Romy within the cloud of their rainbow green light.

...

Cherry stares on at Remy's sleeping face for a long time, losing herself in a trance of tender desire. 'When he is asleep like this he is mine,' she mumbles. 'He can only be mine. I know that in the depths of my heart. When will he know? Ah, but he is mine now. Oh, how beautiful he is. Now I must wake him and lose him again.' She blinks rapidly to brush away the moisture that is filling her eyes and, barely moving, her lips descended gently onto one of Remy's closed eyelids and remained there, warm and full bodied, cushioning the eyeball. After an age the lips imperceptibly retreat from the eyelid, the skins clinging for a moment then releasing, and gliding gradually over to the other eye, hover down on that eyelid. There is a moment of absolute stillness then Cherry's face slowly lifts. Her rouge hair brushes Remy's cheeks as she withdraws. Her face remains a short distance away from his, gazing down placidly and gently, replete with unbounded patience.

Everything remains still, then lazily Remy's eyelids flutter, flutter again and open. The black eyes gaze into the green ones above him showing no emotion other than total acceptance.

...

After this Romy decides he must try to face the world.

...

Emilia looks at Romy with wonder. At one glance she sees him as an adolescent and at another as a child. Still slight of frame, he is now taller than her by half a head. His features have refined around the large blue pools of his eyes but his face has remained of soft skin over gentle flesh and delicate bone. His long black hair and the cinders of his brows and lashes highlight his pale complexion. His aura is neither masculine nor feminine but a mirroring of both that makes people catch their breath and stare when first they see him.

...

From now on Romy ceases to age, and in the way Emilia just saw him he remains the rest of his living days, as ageless as the glen he retreats to as into a womb.

...

'Son, do you think you should go alone? What happens if you have one of your attacks? Who will be there for you?' John asks Romy.

'I must go with him,' Remy puts in softly.

'But son,' John said, 'perhaps there are things you want to do for yourself.'

'Romy is myself, Papi. My life is simple, Papi. I live for Romy. I am here to do his will. I am here to help him through this existence. I must go with him. I would never know peace if he was far away and needing me.'

'Very well, son, you must both go. I'm glad Romy won't be alone.'

Cherry, who has been forgotten by John and Emilia during this exchange, speaks up now with determination. 'I will go too,' she says.

'But Cherry,' John says, 'Romy and Remy are tied by bonds of brotherhood and love and by something spiritual that came with them from beyond, but you are free to live your own life. To marry. To have children. To do what you must to become a full blown woman in every way.'

'You're right, Mr Stuart. But things have happened while we have been growing up that have made the three of us one, and now I have slept with one of them on either side of me in the peace of the green light which comes from the blue light of Romy and the yellow light of Remy.'

...

But Romy insists he will go alone, that he will wander with his Gitano family, and that he will come back to the glen and be a shepherd like his father. Remy declares he will go into the army to train and then go out into the world to try to give any little help he can anywhere

...

Cherry's mind shouts out in her head: 'I want Remy! I want to be with him. I want to be his woman and I want him to be my man. I want to bask in the glow of his yellow light and I want him to bask in the light of my love for him. And I want him and me to be with Romy, the three of us alone forever.'

But no one hears these inner shouts except Cherry, and instead she says, 'Well, Mrs Stuart, if Remy is going to go into the army, I think I had better become a nurse. Every warrior needs a nurse, don't you think?'

'And perhaps every nurse needs a warrior,' Emilia says, divining some of Cherry's feelings. 'It is my own profession, child, and it is a beautiful one...'

...

The conflicting sexual impulses and urges and the nature of the love between Romy, Remy and Cherry goes through a rocky run.

Romy is asexual and does not feel romantic and sexual love, only spiritual and charitable love. Cherry loves and desires Remy.

Remy loves Cherry strictly in a sisterly way and has no sexual attraction for her at all.

Remy does, though, have strong sexual urges. He is very sexually attracted to a beautiful and very unconsciously erotic blonde haired girl at school called Jill. Remy is so blind to Cherry's love for him that he actually gets Cherry to set him up with Jill.

He and Jill have an uncontrolled, engulfing fusion of bodies on a pile of sails in the boatshed, while the reflecting waves flit on the walls and ceiling and rock the hulls beside them.

But Remy is unable, unable to enter where life suddenly comes to rest in peace and bliss, unable to finish that which is life fulfilled... unable to betray himself. With every fibre of his being screaming, he rolls off Jill and lies panting beside her, twitching.

This happens soon after the final cricket match, on the sunny Summer evening of sports day, which is the concluding event of their last term at school. Remy has been in all the Olympic events and has won many of them, and is pumped.

He feels very bad about himself after his dizzying encounter with Jill... bad about doing it... bad about not doing it. Great guilt for betraying his spiritual union with Romy and Cherry overwhelms him, and he swears off, but it takes many more clandestine, crushing, inconclusive encounters with Jill for him to become thoroughly disgusted with himself and unable to bear Jill's utter bafflement.

Cherry suffers greatly throughout all this, knowing, but never believing, that she can never have Remy. She has the struggles of her natural desires and affections later on during her time at nursing school, but remains a virgin.

...

When their trinity assumes its adulthood, all three of them are celibate.

...

Romy retains his adolescent appearance and heartrending ethereal beauty. Slight, his white body slim and tender. Lines of expression are totally absent from his gentle pale face, which remains smooth and hairless, wearing only its usual vaguely vulnerable appearance as his large innocent eyes, now more violet than blue, peer from within the backdrop of his long black hair and dark brows.

Remy's figure is now broadening and filling out as it takes on the form of young manhood; and although it remains spare as a whole, his shoulders are broader and the triangle of his grooved torso sits with more prominence on his narrow waist. His hips, seeming slimmer in contrast, are better defined by the butterfly arch of their bones, and firm round buttocks give way smoothly to longer, stronger, more rigidly muscled legs. The features of his face have set into a wel defined mould, remaining fine and sculpted but stronger and more masculine; and blonde fur lies lightly on his jowls. The short bristly hair of his head gives him a fresh and bright aspect. His happy flashing smile shines out ceaselessly, and his golden aura radiates as ever around his black eyes which resemble cooling rocks of lava. However, seriousness and firmness of purpose now make the muscles of his triangular jaw tighten and relax from time to time, and lines expressing determination and strong character are making their appearance on his face.

...

Cherry comes running breathlessly up to John and Emilia, her face beautifully flushed from her excitement and the warmth of the day. 'Oh, hello Mr and Mrs Stuart,' she gasps, flopping down onto the picnic rug spread on the grass outside the boundary of the cricket pitch. Green eyes, bouncing dark red hair, marbled white peachy skin and ripe cherry lips, the features shaping themselves now into their definite form, emerging from alabaster with the serenity of a female Roman bust, so beautiful that they paralyse the viewer's eyes. Her slim swelling body flung around so carelessly makes John's heart miss a beat and to feel a hollow sensation in his abdomen.

...

They are all at the final cricket match for the national public school cup.

Romy. who goes to play some of the sports at the school, and Remy bat together... long and graceful and sweeping and sure, being as mirrors of each other in their gliding play.

Cherry bats with Remy after Romy lets himself be caught out in order to let that happen.

...

She looks deep into Romy's familiar and reassuring eyes. He smiles and says, 'Remy will see you through a few overs.'

'Oh, you knew. I knew you would.'

'Yes, Cherry, I knew.'

'I so wanted to bat with him. Thanks, Romy,'

'That's all right. Well, go on, Remy's waiting for you.'

'O, wow,' she exhales, and raising her head proudly, she flounces out into the thick of the polite fray on the rich, dark green, in the sparkling sunlight from the shining blue sky of a northern Summer afternoon.

...

In order to give the visiting team a chance, later Remy too lets himself be got out.

Towards the end of the game, when Romy and Remy's school are fielding and the other side is batting, the other side's last player emerges onto the field to bat.

...

His legs are half the size of normal legs, so his pads come up to his waist and he dips deeply sideways at every step. His bat is far too long for him, coming up almost to his chest, but he comes on gamely with a happy smile on his face and an attitude of absolute good sportsmanship, taking himself lightly and modestly as though life was a good joke. From the spectators there rises a resounding round of applause and occasional cheers.

Romy and Remy can soon see his huge meaty round face with beady eyes, and that his shoulders are massive and his arms thicker than many people's legs.

'I'll bet he can really hit the ball if he can connect,' Remy says...

Romy and Remy will not bowl him out, but the deformed boy senses this and taunts and makes fun of them both for it, grotesquely larking around the wicket between overs to the great amusement of the crowd. Finally Romy and Remy understand that he doesn't want any special treatment, and the boy bats his team to victory from a shot which leaves him sprawling on the ground as the ball bounces over a fielder's boot and across the boundary.

Romy and Remy rush to pick him up. Now,' the boy says, 'give me your arms and help me walk off because I'm very tired and I don't want people to make a fuss.' And linking his arms with Romy and Remy's, the three of them walk off the cricket field looking like the angels of day and night bearing up a giant, lame toad.

...

Remy asks Romy to help this boy, Donald, so horribly deformed by polio. But Romy says that the boy has already found his interior beauty for himself, about which Donald tells them in a dream-like, drawn-out, far away tale.

Disgusted by his fate and that all his relationships can only be artificial ones, Donald had a near death experience from an overdose of sleeping pills his mother had been prescribed.

...

'Life becomes a permanent stare down the disappearing dark hole of an existence which is nothing but an unending cycle of sickening unhappiness and despair. The last thing to go is hope. Even after faith had gone, I still hoped. I hoped for the impossible, and then a wave of reality came over me and a still quiet darkness closed in on me and I knew it was the end. I was resigned to my fate now. There was no going back.

'I loved my life at the very end and I knew that I had done something that went against the divine rule of nature. I had cut short the time of my life. I had not learned all that I should have learned in this life, and there was silent disapproval in heaven and throughout all creation.

'Then I cried out, "No, God, please no! I didn't know. I didn't understand. Give me another chance."'

'It was my first step to salvation even though it had burst from me of its own accord, even though I thought then that it was hopeless.

'A long time passed, yet I was instantly engulfed by pure still white light. I became pure white light existing within pure white light. Then I saw, yet I didn't see. I just knew. I somehow felt I was within others and others were within me and those others were my ancestors. I knew them all although I'd never seen them even in photographs, and they gathered round me and inside me and I moved in and around them and there was great joy and gladness and I heard yet I didn't hear - I just knew that they were wishing me welcome. They were dancing and singing within me and letting me know how happy they were that I had joined them. I felt like I'd come home. A great sense of homecoming came over me and I let them sweep me along until a greater light yet descended on me, this time of crystal clarity; or maybe I moved into it, I don't know, but I was suddenly alone again, yet I was overcome by sound, sound was all around me and inside me, or was it just the feeling of sound? I don't know, but it seemed to merge with me, and, as though I was speaking to myself, as though I was thinking it for myself or as though I understood all thought at one thought, it said to me: "It is not time yet. Your time has not come. You must go back."

'Oh, but it's so beautiful here. It's so tranquil,' I thought, or in some other way relayed my feelings. 'I breathe love here. Love is in me and all around me and I am filled with sheer delight.'

'"You must go back." And voices echoed in my head. My own voice, voices I knew, voices I didn't, voices of children and old men, women's voices, all talking at different tempos, all talking at the same time, getting louder and louder:

"You're right. You must go back. Yes, I'm right, you must go back. Yes, you must return. You have not finished. You and I have not finished. Yes, we must go back. We must finish what has to be finished. Then they will bring you back. They, you, I will bring me back. I, you, they will bring us back. We will bring thou back. I will be thou. Thou will be them. I am!"'

Donald nearly shouted this last affirmation. Then he calmed and went on: 'I was confused and a little frightened by the ruckus but then I realised the truth of it. You see, there was no I. There was no you. There was no we or them. There was just one, and I was one with The One.

'My confusion and fright lasted only until I realised this, and then there was only The One Voice speaking softly and firmly and full of warmth, and it was the voice of my mother, and she said to me, "Donald, my beloved, grace be unto you, and peace."'

'I couldn't believe my ears,' Donald exalted. 'My heart swelled with joy and relief. "Mummy, I'm so glad you're here," I said in wonder. "Oh, speak to me, Mummy."

"Beloved of mine, this is the season of your darkest hour and here is the purpose to your flight:

Your old self has died, now you shall be reborn; you have planted your suffering, now you shall pluck;

You have killed your old self, now you shall heal; you have broken down, now you shall build up;

You have wept, now you shall laugh; you have mourned, now you shall dance, for it is not sturdy legs that dance but the spirit;

You have cast stones away, now gather them together; refrain from self-destruction and embrace life;

You shall get, for losing is done with; you shall keep, and cast no more away;

Rend no more, but sew; keep silent no more, but speak your heart;

With love overcome hate; war no more on yourself, but be at peace.

See how God has made all things beautiful for you in your time, for there is no good in them, but for you to rejoice in them, and to do good in your life."

'And I walked unhindered by my deformities. I walked freely and lightly, with spring in my step, and with joy in my heart, and so I have felt ever since.'

After a moment's silence Remy asked: 'You feel this now even though you are still deformed?'

Romy replied for Donald, 'Many are physically sound but many more are spiritually deformed. Now Donald is spiritually sound and therein is true freedom.'

'That's what you did for Cameron and the headmaster, isn't it?' Remy asked Romy.

'Yes,' Romy replied.

'But, like Donald, you didn't have to do anything for the little boy Thomas?'

'No.'

...

The first distant strangers to seek Romy out for help had recently arrived on foot at the glen.

...

In the early gloaming Remy had stopped when he saw Romy's figure hurtling towards them on running legs down the path, and now his face lit up with a smile. He was pushing his bike along at his right side and on his shoulders he carried a small boy whose hands were clasping his forehead. To his left, a stooped, strong old man with a seasoned leathery face and thick unruly grey hair, dressed in rough farming clothes and with a satchel hanging down his back, was gamely pushing himself forward with a gnarled shepherd's crook.

Totally unaware of Remy's companions, Romy's pent up emotions gushed from him, 'Oh Remy, I was so worried. I was so worried.'

'I knew you would be, Romy, but I'm here now. I'm here now, so don't be upset. I'm late because I met up with these people who were coming to see you.'

Romy's gaze had shifted to the young boy on Remy's shoulders and he stood transfixed by him, gaping at him with reverence.

'This is Thomas,' Remy said.

The boy was about six years old. His head was completely bare of hair, the skull saved from the skeleton only by the tender spongy white scalp lining the dome of his seemingly outsized cranium and by the thin transparent veneer of bluish skin covering the sharp protuberances of his facial bone structure, from out of which the enormous spheres of his gelatinous dark eyes pulsed with a low frequency.

His body and limbs were mere figments of substance beneath loose, hanging clothes, and his entwined fingers over Remy's forehead were shrivelled and as white as the underlying bones, with translucent nails the colour of bruised flesh.

The boy gazed back at Romy and gently their souls merged.

Remy and the old man, Jock, the little boy's grandfather, watched them compassionately... Remy knowingly, the old man hopefully.

From the recesses of his entrancement Thomas said in a clear treble voice, 'Hello, Romy.'

'Hello, Thomas,' Romy said.

'I've come to be with you when I die.'

'I know,' Romy said, and they continued their benevolent gaze.

'Oh, Thomas, oh, Thomas,' Romy whispered brokenly.

Jock raised his voice, 'No, no, no Thomas, son, that's no' the way o' it, lad. We've come so that Romy can heal you. Romy lad, we're awfy glad tae see you, son. We've come an awfy long way.'

With a colossal effort Romy brought himself under control and brusquely brushed away the tears before bringing the small body down from Remy's shoulders and gently cradling it in his arms.

Thomas looked up at him and said openly and innocently, 'I've got a brain tumour and my Mummy and Daddy died in a car crash.'

Darkness swirled around Romy. His shoulders shook uncontrollably twice and because he knew he would be unable to speak, he only bent and kissed Thomas on his cold forehead.

'Don't be sad, Romy,' Thomas said. 'I'm going to heaven soon and then everything will be all right.'

'Yes, Thomas,' Romy managed to croak.

'I've been waiting,' Thomas said.

'Waiting for what?' Romy asked almost inaudibly.

'Waiting to find you, Romy.'

'I'm glad you found me, Thomas,' Romy whispered.

Thomas stared passively, entirely surrendering himself to Romy's eyes.

'Oh, it's now or never!' Romy gasped.

'Don't do it!'Remy almost ordered, and Romy's eyes leapt to his, screaming at him in noiseless agony for an instant.

'Look at him, Remy. Look at him,' Romy sobbed loudly. 'He needs me, Remy. He needs me.'

'No he doesn't!' Remy shouted. 'He's still in God's hands and you know it. You're not allowed to heal the body, only the spirit. You know that. You know that.'

"But I've got to try, Remy," Romy wailed. "I've got to try or I'll die.'

'Hold me,' Romy gasped, and Remy quickly clasped him firmly around the shoulders with one strong arm.

'I'm ready...' Remy began to say but his arm was instantly wrenched away as Romy's body suddenly jerked up and back with a force far beyond his strength and his head was flung over his shoulders so that his face looked straight up into the boiling night shrouded clouds with fixed staring eyes.

Romy's legs abruptly folded under him, and as though floating down, he crumpled to the ground supported by Remy, and Thomas sank into his lap.

'Son, what's happenin'?' Jock whispered to Remy as Remy strained to keep Romy's body up. 'Is Thomas dead?'

'No,' Remy replied.

'Well, what is it then? Is this the miracle? Is Romy healin' Thomas now?'

'I don't know,' Remy said. 'He's trying to do something he shouldn't.'

Then they saw that Romy's eyes bulged and stared crazily and out of focus at nothing other than in on himself, and from out of his gaping mouth a screeching cracked and gurgling scream burst so suddenly and loudly that roosting crows exploded into the dark overcast sky and cawed madly, and Remy and the old man froze as though turned into pillars of salt.

The dying daylight flared and flagged, flared and flagged, jumping all things from outsized to downsized, thrusting forward and ripping back the stark dark silhouette of the looming mountains in the distance, and off roofs of slate and chimney blocks, off rocky walls of velvet black the glaring paddocks round, off the glassy molasses stream swiftly running by, and off the jagged teeming trees both near and far, and there, amid, the cringing huddle of age-old man and twain of twin in youth and little child as though slain.

Then suddenly all was dark and black as pitch and Remy and the old man stood rooted in tense anticipation as the start of a distant chilling wail came to them from out of the oppressive darkness. Eerily and unrelentingly it grew in intensity, whistling and shrieking and rebounding off the mountainsides around them, making the trees to groan and sigh and their hair to rise up on their scalps until they could bare it no longer and were forced to stop up their ears with the palms of their hands before the onslaught of the final defining crescendo.

Quicker than it had come it was gone, and in its wake there was a mighty crack followed by a long repeating peal of rumbling booming thunder which reluctantly and lingeringly died away, and then all momentum was stayed and there remained only the whispering static of the still small voice.

Remy hugged Romy, 'I'm here, Romy. I'm here. Everything's all right, Romy. Everything's all right now.'

'Remy, I can't open my eyes.'

'Your eyes are open, Romy.'

'No they're not, Remy. They can't be, Remy. Open my eyelids with your fingers, Remy.'

'Your eyes are open, Romy.'

'Oh, Remy, I'm blind. I'm blind!'

Remy's face contorted and tears welled up in his eyes and ran silently down his cheeks.

'Why did you do it? Why did you do it?' he shouted angrily. 'You stupid idiot. You're so stupid sometimes.Now look what's happened. Do you see what you've done? I can't help you this time, you know? You know that, don't you, don't you?' he gasped, and then great sobs burst from him and he knelt there before his sightless beloved brother.

'Remy, I'm scared, I'm scared, I'm so scared. I'm sorry, I'm so sorry.'

But Remy's heaving dry sobs continued uncontrollably and he lifted his head to the night sky and screamed out in agony,

'I love him more than I love you, God. Do you hear me? I love him more, much more. Greater love is not possible. Do you hear me? Do you hate us so much? Do you hate us two pathetic little beings so much that you would make even the greatest of loves as nothing? You don't know love at all. You don't know love as I do. If you did you wouldn't always want to be the high and mighty one. That's all you care about. All you care about is being top dog, and you don't care who you trample on to prove you are. Leave us alone from now on, do you hear me? Leave us alone, alone!'

Then out of the taut silence Thomas' high weak voice sang out, 'Don't be angry with God, Remy. Don't be sad. Don't cry any more. I'll make Romy better when I go to heaven. I'll ask God to forgive him and He will make him better.'

Remy's body came to rest and he stared at Thomas as hope stirred in him and began to revive his spirit. After a long silence he said, 'Do you think you can, Thomas? Do you really think you can?'

Two shafts of light passed momentarily over their heads from the yellow headlights of the old four-wheel drive as it lumbered towards them.

Remy turned hastily to Romy and asked him hurriedly in an undertone, 'What are we going to say?'

But Romy's head was hanging down and he was sound asleep.

...

Outside the door of the bedroom where Romy slept on, Remy looked at Thomas and put a silencing finger to his mouth. He opened the door and without turning on the light pulled Thomas in after him and closed the door.

'Can't we turn on just one light?' Thomas asked in a whisper.

'Shh,' Remy whispered. 'Look.'

'Where?' Thomas asked.

'Just look straight ahead.'

'I can't see anything,' Thomas whispered again.

'You will,' Remy said. 'Just keep looking.'

After a pause of absolute quiet and stillness, Thomas said in quiet amazement, 'Oh it's so beautiful. It's so beautiful. I want to go into it. Can I go into it, Remy?'

'Yes, Thomas,' Remy said softly. 'You above all others can do whatever you want.'

Thomas stayed stock still for a while letting his eyes absorb the arc of misty blue spangled light over Romy's silent body.

'Oh, it's so beautiful,' he breathed again and slowly edged over towards the glow. When he was near enough he tentatively reached out his hand and slipped it into the soft light and as he did he took in a sharp breath and hastily pulled his hand back. 'Oh, I felt my heart jump for joy, Remy,' he said in wonder.

'Go all the way in,' Remy said, 'and you will know what you will feel like in heaven.'

And there in Romy's heavenly light Thomas stayed until Remy had to say, 'Come now, sweet Thomas, enough. Let's get you into bed.'

Remy laid Thomas in his own bed beside Romy's, and as he left the room, when he switched off the light, he knew that soon Thomas would be able to see Romy's light again.

Thomas lay on in the darkness with the blue glow beside him. He knew he was the only one awake in the house.

He basked in the radiance of wellbeing coming from Romy's light and his thoughts took leave of him and wandered along their own paths.

'Is that you, Thomas?' a voice spoke out of the darkness, making Thomas' heart jump with fright before he realised that it was Romy speaking and that the change he had been searching for was that Romy's light had gone out.

'Yes, Romy.'

'Thomas,' Romy said, 'will you look out the window and tell me what kind of night it is?'

Thomas got up and looked out the window. 'It's a beautiful night, Romy,' he said. 'There isn't a cloud in the sky and there is a full moon and lots and lots of pale stars. All the fields look as though the grass is made of silver and the walls and the trees and bushes are all made of silver and there is so much light I can see the sheep like balls of cotton in the fields. And I can see right up to the top of the glen. Oh, there's a stream glinting in the moonlight, Romy, and a waterfall right at the top of the glen that looks like a silver ribbon hanging down the black crags. Oh Romy, everything is so beautiful that I wish I could be out there so that the moon would shine on me and I could feel as beautiful as everything else.'

'You will, Thomas. Let's go,' Romy said, eagerly throwing off his bed covers. 'There is something I want to show you too.'

'Oh really, Romy, what is it?'

'Wait and see,' Romy said. 'It's a surprise. Take my hand now. Are you sure it's bright enough to see without a torch?'

'Oh yes,' Thomas replied.

'Do you see a roomy shed on a small knoll over there to the left behind the farmhouse buildings? Well, that's where we're going,' Romy said, and soon two spectral figures crossed the courtyard, the short one trailing the tall one.

When they got into the shed Romy asked, 'Are you ready, Thomas?' and threw the light switch.

All was bathed in fluorescence.

'Oh wow,' Thomas at last breathed in amazement as he stared at the two cavernous skeletal structures that towered over him.

'They're wagons!' he exclaimed. 'Just like the ones of the wild west. Oh Romy,' he gasped, 'the sides are all carved with trees and fruits and flowers. Oh look, there are birds and deer. Oh, Romy, this so beautiful. Who did it? Was it you?'

'Yes, Thomas,' Romy said happily, 'I'm so glad you like it. Just imagine what the caravans will look like when the rest of the carvings are painted.'

'Oh how I wish I could see that. Did you build the wagons as well?'

'Well, Romy and I and my father did, but I did all the carvings. And Cherry, the beloved third one, helped. Now come over here and take us into that room over there.'

Thomas hesitated then took them into the dark room.

'Ready?' Romy said.

'Yes,' Thomas said.

Romy threw the light switch and again Thomas stood rooted to the spot while he gaped at what was revealed.

A few paces before his eyes were four open-sided stalls and in each stood a massive majestic horse, passively chewing, completely unruffled by the late night intrusion.

'Wow! Oh wow!' Thomas gasped. 'I've never seen such big horses. I could walk right under one without ducking. Oh, Romy, what are their names?'

'Well,' Romy said, 'they are Clydesdale horses, and from left to right their names are Dasher, Dancer, Prancer and Vixen.'

'Oh, you've named them after Santa's reindeer!' Thomas exclaimed, 'Oh, all this is so wonderful and exciting that I feel like it really is Christmas. Oh Romy, I don't want to go to heaven now. I want to stay here with you and Remy so that you can teach me how to carve and so that I can go riding, and when I don't feel well I can stand in your lights and get better.' And he threw himself onto Prancer, hugging one of his legs, and Romy could hear his muffled weeping.

Romy swallowed, holding back his own tears, and with a catch in his voice said as cheerily as he could, 'Come on, Thomas, I've got something else to show you. We're going to my workshop.'

The workshop had a cosy, protective atmosphere and Thomas immediately felt a gentle peace descend on him. There was a panel on one wall bearing a selected array of clean, effective looking tools of lustrous metal and warm wood. The other walls had shelves holding a selection of carvings and Thomas took in at a glance a flower, several of birds, one of a tree, another of a waterfall, one of a horse rearing up and one of a shepherd with a sheep in his arms and a crook in his hand.

Then, as though out of the furthest reaches of eternity, distinct clear notes materialised in the air around them, each one an individually, perfectly created crystalline drop bursting in briefly expanding concentric circles.

'Beethoven for you, Thomas,' Romy said, staring unseeingly. 'But it's I who has never heard music in this way before. I'm seeing music with my ears. Thomas, are you there?

Thomas moved to Romy's side. 'Oh, Romy, I'm scared. I'm scared that there won't be any of these things in heaven. I don't think I could bear it if I could never have any of these things again. Will you be able to carve in heaven? Will the man who made this music be able to make more music in heaven? I don't see how heaven can be more beautiful than the world. I don't see how there can be more beautiful music in heaven than the music we're listening to. Oh Romy, I didn't really see. I didn't really hear, and now it's too late. Oh. Romy, I'm scared of heaven.'

Romy hugged Thomas to him tightly.

'Don't be sad, little one,' Romy said. 'I understand fear of heaven. What if all we want to do when we get to heaven is to come back to our home on earth? Even you who have only known suffering feel you will miss your earthly life. Even you, who have never sinned yet have been through hell here on earth, are loath to go.'

'But I've known happiness too,' Thomas said. 'This has been the most beautiful day of my life Romy.'

Romy said, 'You know that all children have their angel in heaven. Your angel is waiting for you.'

'Oh, Romy, you're right,' Thomas said eagerly. 'I do have an angel. I know she is there. I can feel her. I've never seen her but I can feel her. Oh, I can't wait to see her Romy. I can't wait for her to hug me.'

'In that case, it's time for your next surprise,' Romy said secretively.

'Oh, what is it, Romy?'

'Are your eyes open?' Romy asked.

'Yes,' Thomas said.

'All right, take this cover away,' Romy said, reaching out to a draped object near to him on the workbench.

Thomas took the cover in his hand and said, 'I'm ready.'

'All right,' Romy said, 'Do it.'

Thomas solemnly dragged the sheet down until it dropped onto the workbench and he looked in disbelief at the revealed figure.

'It's my angel,' he whispered. 'It's my angel, Romy. You've made my angel for me. I've seen her at last. Oh Romy, isn't she beautiful? Isn't she the most beautiful angel of all?'

After a long wait Thomas hypnotically reached out a hand and set it down softly on the angel's feet, and as it came to rest a peaceful smile illuminated his face and his eyes shone with infinite patience and absolute forgiveness, and time throughout all of creation was measured by his heartbeat.

'Oh, Romy,' he whispered, 'Romy, she smiled at me.'

'You can pick her up when we come down the mountain,' Romy said.

'Are we going up the mountain?' Thomas asked incredulously.

'Yes, we're going up to the waterfall.'

'Oh how exciting. It looks so beautiful. But before we go, Romy, won't you tell me who Cherry is and what the caravans are for?'

'Well,' Romy said, 'Cherry is a girl. Remy and I have known her since we were little and she's our other self. She's sort of like a sister but she likes Remy in a different way too.'

'More than she likes you.'

'No,' Romy said thoughtfully, 'just in a different way.'

'Are they going to marry?' Thomas asked impishly.

'They can't marry. Not for a long time anyway.'

'Why not?'

'Remy has to do some things first.'

'What sort of things?'

'Things I can't do myself.'

'Why can't you do them?'

'Because I can't stand the pain.'

'What pain?'

'The pain of life. The pain of all suffering.'

'How do you know you can't stand it? You were able to stand my pain. You fought for me so strongly that God had to blind you.'

'Yes, I fought for you, Thomas, but I don't think I can fight for all of humanity. I don't think I can stand the suffering of the world. Anyway that's what the caravans are for. I'm going to go out into the world to try and find the truth of my existence. I'm going to see how much pain and suffering I can bear.'

'And you're going with Remy and Cherry?'

'No, I must try alone. Up to now when I can't stand the pain and I try to go away it has been Remy who brings me back, and Cherry was able to do it once too. But we must go our own ways now and come back to each other on the other side of life.'

'Where will you be going?'

'All over Europe. You see, my grandparents are Gitanos... Gypsies, and I am to travel with their village caravan in the ones you saw.'

'They're Gypsies!' Thomas exclaimed. 'Oh, how exciting. Oh Romy, can I go? Oh, I'd forgotten. I'm going to heaven. But Romy, if I haven't gone when it's time for your trip, can I go with you?'

'Of course you can, Thomas,' Romy said. 'Of course you can.'

'Oh, I'm not going to go to heaven,' Thomas said with bravado. 'I'm going to fight like you fought for me, Romy, and I'm going to stay.'

Romy looked out at nothing and blinked rapidly.

'You don't believe me, do you, Romy?' Thomas said challengingly. "But I am, I'm going to fight to stay and go on the trip with you. Come on, I'll show you how tough I am. Let's go up to the waterfall.' He went over to Romy and took him by the hand.

'Thomas,' Romy said, 'if you're coming on the trip with me, let me show you where you're going to sleep.'

'Really,' Thomas gasped. 'Oh, show me.'

And so, with Thomas leading, they went through to the room the caravans were in and Romy said, 'The one on the right is the sleeping caravan. Climb in.'

'Oh yes,' Thomas said eagerly. 'I can see the bunk beds,' and he dragged himself up into the caravan. 'Can I sleep on the top bunk Romy? Oh please.'

'Yes you can,' Romy said. 'Don't you want to go up to the waterfall any more?'

'Oh yes,' Thomas exclaimed. 'I'd forgotten.' And he clambered down off the caravan.

Back on the ground he eagerly grabbed Romy's hand and said, 'Let's go,' and outside they went.

'Look up the glen, Thomas,' Romy said.

'I am,' Thomas replied.

'All right, do you see the ridge that runs up the right hand of the glen to the top of the waterfall?'

'Yes. Are we going to go right to the top of the waterfall?'

'Yes,' Romy said.

'Oh, that's just what I was hoping for,' Thomas said excitedly. 'Can we look over the top of the waterfall and see the water splashing down?'

'Yes we can, Thomas,' Romy said.

As they were passing the orchard Thomas saw the family graveyard through the tress.

'Who's buried in that graveyard, Romy?' he asked.

'My forefathers on my father's side,' Romy said.

Thickly, Thomas asked, 'Where will you and Remy be buried? Oh tell me that I can be buried in that corner with you and Remy.'

'I tell you with absolute assurance that your place will be between Remy and me, and we three shall lie there in peace and brotherly love for ever, and until Remy and I join you we will come and be with you from time to time.'

...

"Is then the die cast, O Mother Moon, that your light was only shed to show inevitable doom? Shame on you, O Mother Moon, Shame on you, and upon you be all the blame!"

...

Romy squeezed Thomas' little hand in his.

'Come away now, little brother, for we have a ways to go yet.'

And hand in hand they turned and walked on silently.

Then Thomas said excitedly, 'Romy, Romy, I know what we'll do. I'll walk ahead of you whistling and you can follow the sound. Why, I'll whistle, "When the saints go marching in."'

So the jolly carefree moment progressed. Thomas was as light as a feather and as free as the wind whistling along, and Romy happily advanced behind filled with delight at the child's joy.

'Oh, I'm out of breath,' Thomas gasped when they were high up the ridge leading to the waterfall.

He threw himself down on the grassy ground, panting.

Their breathing slowly settled and Thomas sat up and looked delightedly around him.

'Oh, Romy I didn't know it was possible to be so happy. I never knew before just how beautiful everything is.'

Then, suddenly, everything went black before him and a blinding flash of light tore at the retinas of his eyes and his whole body jumped as every muscle constricted at once. The phenomenon was over in an instant and Thomas looked around in fear and bafflement.

Feeling tension in the atmosphere, Romy asked, 'Are you all right, Thomas?'

'Oh yes, Romy, I'm fine.' Thomas replied.

'Are you sure?' Romy insisted.

'Oh yes,' Thomas said. 'Shall we move on?'

'Yes, let's go,' Romy said. 'We want to get to the top before the moon goes down.'

Romy understood that something was not right but he took Thomas's hand and remained silent and thoughtful.

After trudging forward for a while Romy suddenly felt Thomas' hand snatched from his and heard the dull thud of Thomas' body falling to the ground. He immediately threw himself down after Thomas, and groping around he touched Thomas' shoe. He felt his way up the emaciated body, realising as he did so that his mind had blocked out the extent of Thomas' physical degeneration and he felt infinitely sad to have returned to the truth.

He rolled Thomas over and when he ran his fingers over Thomas' face to determine his condition they froze as they touched the wetness of tears running down the sharp, small bony face.

'What's happening, Thomas?' he asked pleadingly. 'Tell me. You must tell me.'

'Oh Romy, I'm not going to make it to the top of the glen. I'm not going to make it, Romy,' Thomas sobbed, then went as limp and still and silent as darkness.

Romy took the little face in the palms of his hands and lowered his mouth to the ear nearest to him. 'Thomas,' he whispered, 'I'll get you to the top of the glen if it's the last thing I do.' And reaching one arm under Thomas' neck and the other under the back of his knees, he braced himself and rose with the scraggy frail body in his arms.

Then, taking a few tentative steps to determine which way was up, he set off strongly, determined to reach his destination, if not by sight, then by brute force.

He soon lost all contact with the narrow path and forged on through long grass and thick short heather. He just kept going up.

Drenched in sweat his face and hands became scratched and cut, and his trousers were torn at the knees and the cloth there flapped around bloody skin. His hands were bloody too from breaking his repeated falls on the coarse ground and his hair became tangled and streaked with dust which turned to mud in his sweat.

Soon he realised that he had entirely lost his bearings and the undergrowth suddenly became thicker and rougher, but he would not stop, and instead turned Thomas and his back to it and forced his way, pushing and elbowing backwards, further and further into it until he could hardly move forward at all, and his sobbing became dry coughs and whining moans.

When he was about to surrender to hopelessness and let himself sink to the ground, he heard sweet high words coming to him from out of his darkness as from another world.

'You're miles off the track!'

There was a long silence then Romy asked, 'Is that you, Thomas?'

'Yes,' Thomas said.

'Thomas, Thomas, I thought I'd never hear you again. Oh, what a relief. I was trying to get you to the top of the glen because I knew you wanted to get there more than anything.'

'Oh Romy, I love you. I love you,' and Thomas reached up with his slender arms and hugged Romy tightly round his neck and Romy lifted and hugged Thomas' body into his own.

'Romy, we're in the middle of a gorse thicket,' Thomas said.

'Do you still want to go to the top of the glen, Thomas?' Romy asked.

'Yes,' Thomas said. 'Very much. It's all I want to do now.'

'All right,' Romy said. 'How long do you think the moon will last?'

'I don't know, but it's sinking.'

'All right, we'll just have to hope for the best. Lead us on, Thomas.'

'All right, Romy, but if I pass out again wait for me to recover this time.'

'I will, Thomas.'

They staggered up the rest of the ridge then into a small shallow valley and stopped by the stream a little before it poured over the crag and became the long, tumbling waterfall.

Romy gently laid Thomas down on the ground and threw himself gratefully down beside him.

The moon was very low on the high horizon of mountaintops behind them, and after a short rest Romy asked, 'Do you want to go and look over the top of the waterfall?'

There was a long silence before Thomas said, 'I've seen enough, Romy. I've seen all I want to see of this world. I can feel my angel calling me now. I'm sleepy now, Romy. I'm sleepy, Romy, and I'm cold.'

Romy sat up and took off his jacket, reached out for Thomas and lifted him onto his lap. He wrapped Thomas in his jacket so that Thomas was snug and only his face peeked out of the collar of the jacket.

Thomas' eyelids were partially closed and he was smiling sweetly as he gazed with dreamy, blurry eyes at the moon.

But this Romy could not see. 'Thomas, look straight into my eyes,' he said,

'Are you going to take me to meet my angel?' Thomas asked.

'Yes,' Romy replied.

'Oh not yet, Romy. Just a little longer.'

'All right, Thomas,' Romy said. 'All of time past and of time now and all of time forever is yours, Thomas.'

'Oh, I don't need that much, Romy. I only need a few seconds.'

Romy sat still and quiet and full of patience, facing down towards where the sound of Thomas' voice had come, until he heard Thomas say, 'I'm looking into your eyes now, Romy. Thank you for the best, the most wonderful, the most beautiful day... and night of my life. Say goodbye to Grandpa for me and to Remy. Tell them I love them.'

'I will, Thomas.'

'I'm ready now,' Thomas whispered.

Romy bowed his head and kissed Thomas on the forehead. He began to will his sightless way into the weightless, flowing serenity of Thomas' eternally disembodied being, but he was not allowed, and Thomas saw his blank eyes slowly close and his chin sink gently onto his chest.

When Romy's eyes opened a little while later Thomas' soft face was looking serenely back up at him with glazed, gently smiling eyes.

Momentarily confounded, Romy raised his eyes and saw the powerful red dawn emerging over the distances off beyond the farm.

He looked quickly down at Thomas again.

'Goodbye, Romy,' Thomas murmured, and as though blowing out a very small candle, he exhaled for the last time.

The little body collapsed slightly in on itself as the substance of the soul left it.

And the moon rocked on the verge of the mountains before sinking to and fro beneath.

Day Burst! In the Glen

Apart and Alone

So, each driving one of the horse drawn caravans, Romy is taken by John to a fishing vessel Emilia's family have sent to pick him up at a small fishing village with a stone walled harbour on the rough rocky coast.

Emilia's family is waiting for him in Spain. He travels alone with them all over Europe, but mainly Eastern Europe, where East meets West and bloods are clotted and the air breathes the substance of Man's heart and soul flung about in great wonders of beauty and defilement mixed.

He does no healing. He prepares himself. He builds up his spiritual reserves and grows in wisdom - His forty days and forty nights.

Remy goes into the army. He prepares himself. He builds up his defiance and fearlessness of evil - A voice crying in the wilderness of his soul.

Cherry goes to nursing school in Edinburgh, into the sheltering gloominess under its looming Castle and black Cathedral towers, into the dim glow of its cobbled old town, struck between heaven in the glen and earth in the Firth of Forth, teetering emotionally between the spirit and the body - A kneeling handmaiden holding out her open hand.

She is very beautiful, and although she is aware of it, she takes little notice of it. She tries to live up to the forced frantic lives of recently liberated youth and does her best to have romantic and sexual relationships, but she can feel no bond and she will not give herself away. She only feels at home in the operating rooms and the wards, and her affection is for the patients, mainly for the young and mainly for the old; and the hospitals vie for her, but she hardly notices.

Trial and Transition

When Remy finishes his army training he does not go home, but gets work on a cruise ship as a security guard, and he rides the swells.

He leaves ship in a South American country and wanders up the mountains on foot and hitchhiking, overcome now by the craving to deliver himself.

When walking through the shanty suburbs of a large mountain town on the sides of a steep valley, he abruptly turns off the road onto the stony ground of a narrow, deep, lonely alley with walls of bare brick and dry cement and jutting ledges.

Into the *barrio* - where the State does not exist, where the law is unto itself by gun power, where danger presides and there is no hope of help from beyond.

In the alley he hides his cruise ship earned dollars in a hole he digs with his small sheath knife beside the crude column of a bare wall.

...

Cherry finishes her nursing degree and goes home to the school where she becomes the matron and is much loved by the children, especially the little ones; but she scarcely feels the presence of her existence.

...

John dies. He falls off the crag near the cascade trying to rescue a lamb stranded on a ledge.

Emilia buries him in the farm graveyard. She cringes and strains and grits her teeth and screams in her head and walks up and down and round and round in circles for days on end, unseeing, unhearing, unfed.

Romy comes home and holds her, on and on and on until he heals her and peace descends again upon her.

Cameron comes to offer condolences and takes over the running of the farm and lives in the stone and slate attic of the ancient house.

And out of the blue, like a wizard, Donald arrives, and lives in one of the barns, on its mansard.

There is a lull. And then, falteringly, in ones and twos, on foot or dropped off like dumped loads from vehicles which drive quickly away, maybe but a day, maybe weeks or months apart, the lost arrive, waiting outside the farm buildings, the past gone from their eyes, standing there rocking, or sitting on a suitcase, or leaning on a crutch, or one aged mate bearing up the other, or hugging a doll, or bouncing a ball, unannounced, but not unexpected.

They are quietly taken in and quietly enter as though come home. They are fed and washed and the damage to their bodies treated by Emilia and Donald, a lurching goblin, sweating from the effort of moving, shining with subdued laughter.

Romy takes each of them onto his bosom as often as his strength allows him, and their hearts warm and their spirits find peace, some for a year or two, some for an hour.

Romy flutters and flickers as his flame is consumed, but his beauty and youth remain pristine, and he appears ever younger as the others age in toil and dedication and devotion.

As the demands on his energy increase he begins to call out aloud in his sleep for Remy and for Cherry.

Emilia calls Cherry, but none know where Remy is.

With the phone to her ear Cherry sinks onto her knees, reaching out to the wall, a great sob bursting from her when she understands that she is needed in the glen.

She soon arrives, and with Cameron's help she sets up a field hospital, with tents for the children, for boys and for girls, for the aged, for the men, for the women, for the couples, and she and Emilia adopt nurse's uniforms with caps, and latrines are dug and water channelled into shower stalls through water heaters, a refectory, a surgery, a dispensary, a laundry, and to all appearances, beside the farm buildings, a first world war field hospital slowly takes shape, busy and cheery, and there is a sense of discipline and purpose and dignity in its aura, muddy in Spring and Autumn, frozen white in Winter, and carpeted in green in Summer.

And Cherry waits for Remy, in the meantime fulfilled.

Romy will hardly rest and refuses to refuse anyone at any time of day or night. When he is beyond exhaustion Cherry will embrace him and let him sleep in her arms, and she bathes in his blue light celestial, and is the better off of the two.

And Romy pines for Remy, heavy of heart without him.

Agony and Abnegation...

Remy comes out of his long gloomy alley into a more open area, a small, gravelly plaza, solitary at the time, straightens up, and marches over to the "cantina," come store, come restaurant, come bar, come whore house, come anything; open fronted with a flapping canvas canopy and rickety chairs and tables.

From its dark interior a squeaky voice screams out, 'Ey, meester! Joo crayzy?'

It's the cheeky local gamin, Pedro, called Pedrito, who has a saying for every eventuality, like, 'He's more serious than a pig pissing', 'This is harder than a week without meat', 'This is going to be easier than tiger eat banana, "This has more stuff than a cow birthing'.

Pedrito likes speaking English, of which he learned a pigeon version when he and his mother lived and worked in the house of an expatriate family.

'Joo crayzy, meester. Pedrito essaay joo bery crayzy. Dis bery, bery dangeroos place for joo. Dis mor dangeroos dan hornit's nest. Bad, bad peepol here. Dey hurts joo. Dey kills joo. No one helps joo. Everybady bery, bery scared! Drag manny. Mach drag manny. Mach guns. No peety.'

'I will try to change this, Pedrito.'

'Joo bery crayzy. Joo wana die?'

Above the plaza, the rickety, rough, unfinished, uneven brick houses of the middle of the barrio surround a small steep hill, its top flattened to make a dusty playing ground which is starkly illuminated at night by reflectors on posts.

Pedrito's mother runs the cantina and she lets Remy rent a bare brick walled room at the back. She too speaks a little English, so Remy doesn't let on that he speaks Spanish.

He helps out in the cantina and makes it understood that he is a backpacker hitchhiking his way to Patagonia..

He becomes very close to Rosa (Felix), the transvestite whore and whoremaster of the cantina, and takes him to his room regularly, presumably for his services, but actually only to be able to talk freely with him. This also gives him good cover as not being that scrupulous, and he gets a lot of banter about it from the narcos who go to the cantina to eat or drink or relieve themselves. He laughs, as though only understanding the obscene gestures. Really, Rosa (as Felix) is having an intense affair with the striking girl Amanda, one of the cantina's whores.

Felix becomes Remy's dedicated and loyal accomplice. He is tough in a passive, relentless way, emotionally inflexible in the face of threat or for getting what he wants. He too speaks a little

English, learned in a cheap language school down town, because he is to be sent, as a man, out as a mule. He feels trapped and Remy become Rosa's hope of freedom and Felix's hope of salvation, and Rosa and Felix become Remy's hope of liberation by beating the narcos and restoring the barrio to its natural existence.

This he tries to do by secretly inciting the barrio dwellers against the narcos and staging an uprising. Using Pedrito as his cheeky, "unabashable" public relations person, he gets into their houses by offering to teach them English or to help with homework, and soon gets a little school going in a room of wooden boards which he builds up against a wall for the street kids, and also shelters them and feeds and cares for them there.

With his hidden stash of dollars he starts to buy guns using the whores, who become his little army and protect him like a brother or a son. They buy the guns from the narcos' arms dealer, who doesn't want to know who is buying from him, supposedly for barrio narcos, who don't want him to know who is buying from him. Romy hides the guns between the roof tiles and the crude ceiling boards of his room, where only Felix knows they are.

...

The advancing late summer afternoon peace of the glen is shattered by the sudden thunder of three fighter jets streaking though it. They turn far beyond the crag, one to the left, one to the right, and one over itself, and thunder through the glen again, the middle one flying upside down. Crows explode into the air screaming. The fighters begin to circle high and the sound of chopping helicopter blades takes over. A mix of people stream out of the farm buildings and tents and stare up in groups here and there. A large passenger helicopter appears from behind the waterfall and creeps low over the pastures of the glen. Choosing a field, it noisily and blusteringly settles while sheep scatter.

The wide door in the side of the helicopter hull slides opens and a red carpet rolls out onto the grass and a step is lowered onto it. Men in the black garb of priests jump out and line the red carpet.

A small, stooping old man, heavily robed in purple and silver gowns, is helped down and walked to the end of the carpet.

Not understanding, nor thinking it anything to do with them, no one from the farm goes near.

A loudspeaker cracks and squeaks alive and one of the priests says startlingly into a microphone, "Pleese, pleese, here is the living Pope, come for healing of Romy."

A stool is placed behind the Pope and he sits down.

After a long time Romy appears from the farm house with Cherry and they walk across the field up to the sitting old man, made bulky by his glowing gowns.

The Pope is helped to his feet by two black priests, one of whom says: 'You are Romy, the healer of souls, and you are Cherry, the blessed nurse? The living Pope begs Romy to heal him before he dies, for he is much afraid.'

Surrounded now by the ragged happy crowd of the lost, with children on shoulders holding toys and dolls, the old ones leaning on the young ones, Romy looks deep into the Pope's dry brown eyes, seeing not the man but the heart of yet another lost soul.

After a long time, so long the children begin to run around the field and play, Romy says to the Pope, 'I cannot heal you, Sir, but you have nothing to fear.'

On hearing this, the Pope tries to get down onto his knees in front of Romy, but Romy takes him by the arm and holds him up.

'Rather, I ask for your blessing, Sir,' he says, and bows his head. The Pope raises his hand and makes the sign of the cross and mumbles his blessing with tears on his cheeks and a glow of joy on his face.

He glides his raised hand over the crowd of the lost in a general blessing, turns and is helped back into the helicopter, and the black priests pile in behind him, the door closes, the blades rip back to life, and the great hull lifts into the sky and creeps over the crag, and the fighter planes roar away above it.

...

In the mid morning of the day, the four sides of the hot dusty plaza outside the cantina are lined with men holding many types of guns. The slope up to the hilltop playing ground is crowded with barrio dwellers. A deep rumbling emerges from the dark long alley. A block of shadow brushing its walls rocks down it. Silent tension holds until the shadow erupts, belching, into the light of the plaza, a massive burgundy-black security truck for transporting valuables through streets of ultimate danger. Squat, dark, weighing down its wheels with armour plating, small black windows, machine gun barrels poking out of tiny portholes, tracking all around, making those they momentarily point at flinch or duck.

It grinds to a halt in the middle of the plaza, backed up to the crowd on the playing ground hill. From speakers on its flat, hard roof a rough, ruthless voice announces... *'El patrón llega, vecinos. El patrón llega* (The boss arrives, neighbours. The boss arrives).'

The back double doors swing open and four submachine gunned henchmen in black leather jump out and form a semicircle in front of the dark door, and a step appears and is put down from inside.

A figure in pants and shirt steps out - a heavy-set man with a round stomach and a heavy moustache who seems bigger than he is, of quiet, assured demeanour... a man of Napoleonic capacities and daring, holding onto power before his Russian Winter and Waterloo.

He is handed a microphone... '*Vecinos* (Neighbours). Vengo en persona (I come in person) *para decirles* (to tell you) *que entre ustedes* (that among you) *se ha estado cocinando una conspiración en mi contra* (a conspiracy has been cooking against me). *Hago mucho por ustedes* (I do much for you) *y* (and) *me han roto el corazón* (you have broken my heart).' His voice cracks and he shakes his head.

'*¡Queremos ser libres!* (We want to be free!),' the leader of the barrio community shouts out from the slope. '*¡No queremos vivir con miedo siempre!* (We don't want to live with fear always!) *¡Que nuestros hijos estudien y no sean sicarios!* (That our kids study and don't become killers!).'

'*¡Yo sé! ¡Yo sé!* (I know! I know!),' the man almost screams back. '*¡Pero estoy atrapado!* (But I'm trapped!). *Si gano mi guerra los dejo libres* (If I win my war I will let you free).'

'*¡No lo harás!* (You won't do it!),' the leader shouts back. '*¡No podrás nunca!* (You will never be able to!).'

The man rubs his eyes and mumbles chillingly, '*Pues, la batalla hoy es acá* (Well, the battle today is here). *Saquen al muchachito* (Bring out the boy).'

Remy is dragged out of the cantina between two henchmen, his mouth gagged so tight with rope that the sides of his mouth are tearing.

He has been betrayed by Amanda, whom Felix loved too much and trusted too far, but Felix has not told her about the guns.

The Patron, barely glancing at Remy, speaks into the microphone again, '*Vamos a crucificar este muchachito que quiso ser santo* (We are going to crucify this boy who wanted to be a saint). *¡Que no les pase lo mismo!* (May the same thing not happen to you!)'

And the man gets back into the security truck followed by his black leathered guards, who slam the swing doors, and the burgundy-black machine rumbles, belching, back down the alley.

...

In the dusking glen after the living Pope leaves, Romy says he is unable to heal any more.

Emilia asks, 'You mean for today, son?'

'No, Mami. I can never heal again.'

'Why not, *Hijo mío*?'

'Something is happening to Remy, so bad it is breaking the spell. I will go to my room to prepare myself. Please ask Cherry to come and hold me.'

'O, *Hijo*! Please no. Please no, *Hijo*! Not both my beautiful boys at once. Please no! ... Aaa, John, husband and father, be with us now!'

Romy lies down and Cherry takes his head onto her lap and Emilia sits on a chair at the bedside.

Cherry can't contain herself, and despite her resolve to be strong, asks Romy sobbing if Remy will be all right, if he will come back.

'The spell is breaking. It is breaking up,' Romy whispers, eyes closed and terribly pale.

Thus they remain as the hours drag by. The night falls, pitch of night passes, and the painful small hours, and the depressing gray dawn comes, and the day crawls by and by and by, unbearably, and sombre and ghostly creeps the nightfall over again.

...

The sun is blazing down from its zenith onto the shimmering, grimy playing ground atop the hill and into the plaza beneath, and the heat is unbearable.

Solitary in the blinding light from beyond the top of the hill a crude wooden cross made of rough planks, its crossbar crooked, leans sideways.

A slim tender body dressed only in the rags of shorts hangs from it, drooping sideways.

To fasten him to the cross, around Remy's forehead barbed wire has been wound and pulled as tight as possible, and diagonally across his face, crossing over his nose, sparing his eyes, which stare far away, and sparing his mouth, which is forced open, and round his neck and along his arms and round and round his hands and round his shoulders and under his armpits and round and round his chest and waist and under his buttocks and across his crotch, the bulges there horribly mangled, and down each leg and round and round each foot; and blood trickles and stains the whole white body of a sweet innocent boy of perfect youthful beauty.

...

When it is cooler, near sunset, the whores and Pedrito and Rosa walk up the hill to the playing field and silently stand and sit around the cross.

In the glen midnight approaches as black as pitch. With far away looking eyes Romy's head lies in Cherry's lap, spot lit in the dim glow of a bed side lamp.

On the hill, with the last rays of sun haloing his head, Remy croaks, 'Goodbye, Romy,' and gives up his ghost.

In the glen, with the bright material of Cherry's frock haloing his head in the lamplight, Romy hears the gong of the farmhouse grandfather clock loudly strike the first stroke of midnight, and breathes out, 'Remy is dead.'

Unbearable wails break out from Emilia and Cherry. Cherry presses Romy's head to her breast and Emilia throws herself onto his body.

'Romy, not you too, *Hijo*! Romy, stay! Stay! I beg you! Please! Please! *Hijo!*' Emilia desperately pleads.

Cherry moans and moans, 'O, my only two loved ones. My only two loved ones. How can I exist now? How? O, how?'

On the second gong of twelve Romy begins to age, and by each following gong he has aged a year.

'No, no, no. O no. O no,' the women lament, sobbing. 'No, no, no.'

But on the gong of midnight Romy has aged from being an adolescent to a pristinely pure, gently radiating young man.

As the sound of the last gong dies away, he croaks 'Amen,' and his ghost leaves him.

Resolution and Resurrection...

Life is for the living, my dearest ones, for the lively.

The lost continue to come. They make Emilia and Cherry and Cameron and Donald lively in their lives, loving each other and devoted to the ever changing body of the lost.

Jill, the blond beauty of the school, had become a doctor and Cameron persuades her to practise part time at the field hospital as her benevolence, so she lives in the glen some months of the year.

She had been the Marilyn Monroe of the school and none of the moist aura of sexuality breathing from her curved body of perfectly plumb white flesh has been lost - Rather, it has become emphasised. She was never able to commit to another man after her complete surrender to Remy and the pain of that blow to her natural innocence, unintentional as it might have been. But she slowly falls in love with Donald. She cannot understand it. She is far more baffled by this than by her experience with Remy. She fights against it. She tries not to come back to the glen for long spells. But finally she surrenders, again, and finally, for her, to the brim, was peaceful joy; and finally, for Donald also.

Beauty and the Beast, my dearest ones

The Princess and the Frog, my dearest ones.

...

Scrap wood is piled beside the cross. The flies buzz around Remy on it. Gasoline is poured on the wood and a match casually lit and tossed on. Whoosh! A sheet of blue flame blows out. A chainsaw erupts into life and saws through the bottom of the cross. It tilts further, and then drops onto the fire, sparks exploding in a cloud around it, and Remy goes up to heaven in a long winding plume of white smoke.

The community is allowed to use the guns Remy had stashed, which Felix managed to slip, by sleight of hand, to its principals, in order to start their own authorized armed security patrol.

The kids study.

Life is for the alive, my dearest ones.

The barrio is reborn.

A small grotto with a Virgin and babe in arms is built beside the playing ground where Remy died. People leave candles and flowers and lay hands on the babe.

Like Butch and Sundance, the Force guns down the Patron, who stumbles in full view across a Spanish tiled roof to purposely die as he had lived.

Life is for the dying too sometimes, my dearest ones.

...

A gravestone is set for Remy, with Thomas between him and Romy, and John beside them in the farm graveyard.

But abundant life is for those who live again, my dearest ones, and for those who are born.

Cherry and Cameron over time become close in their hearts and when the time is right join their bodies.

...

He looked around, unconsciously registering the time and place; the sun high and dazzling in the vivid, dark blue of the almost indigo sky, rarefied by the contrast of one stark white cloud rising from the top of the steep, solitary glen.

Spilling from the cloud a thin sparkling waterfall splashed down the rocks where the steep black crags that walled in the upper glen joined, and came away as the stream, flashing as it twisted its way down.

Bright, thick purple heather and gleaming coarse yellow broom sway in clumps and tufts at the foot of the black crags, then give way to rough, dark green pastures that spread down, dappled with white patches that blink here and there as the black faced sheep lift and dip their heads in their grazing huddles, the green expanse divided raggedly in two by the stream and carved up randomly like a simple jigsaw puzzle by the winding black stone walls.

Cameron looks along the track that accompanies the stream into the haze far down the long wild valley that eventually merges into the surrounding highlands, no sign of other humanity anywhere, and whispers to himself, 'Beautiful', and turns and wades, dressed only in pants with belt and sheathed knife on, into the pool to stand between Cherry's calves.

A warm cheer goes up from Emilia and Donald and Jill and the muddle of all the lost, leaning out of windows and standing in doors and sitting on the bank below the farmhouse, all within a halo of light, brighter than the day, radiating from their happiness and smiling faces.

In the same waters as Romy and Remy were born, in the same stretch of the same stream, in the same way, Cherry gives birth to twin girls - Romena and Remona.

That night they glow pink in the dark, one white and one red.

I will let you guess which is which, my dearest ones.

And if you are very well behaved I will tell you their story.

Thank you… B.

...